A REVERSE HAREM FANTASY ROMANCE

THE GOLDEN ALICORNS

USA TODAY BESTSELLING AUTHOR

CATHERINE BANKS

To my wonderful husband who introduced me to videogames and anime, two more things for me to destress and obsess over. Thank you for loving this spicy disaster.

The Guild Drafts were finally here and magic hung so heavy in the air that it was a wonder anyone could breathe.

Every town would gather around their town square's screen to watch the drafts live, vendors hawking merchandise for each of the Guilds and food to snack on.

At the Capitol, thousands filled the arena to watch in person as each candidate walked across the stage. The candidates would be scanned and then guilds would choose. Some candidates would have multiple offers and could make their own choice. Each guild's power increased with each member. The more powerful the person, the more powerful the guild and all the members became.

I knew my fate. I registered as having very little magic. No one knew my secret. So, I would likely receive no offers and would have to approach a guild and beg for admittance. I had three choices lined up and my speech already prepared.

Fifty candidates stood in a line, waiting to walk across

the stage. I was near the end, thanks to waking up late and having to run to make it on time.

Three tall, muscular guys stood in front of me. They chatted and laughed about something. How were they so relaxed? They must have been decently powerful and not cared about the outcome … or they had a way into a guild already.

They were similar heights and had the same green eyes, but besides that, they were completely different. So, I didn't think they were brothers. Though, my sister and I looked nothing alike either, so it was still possible.

One of them faced in my direction, the tallest of the group with an aquiline nose, rounded jaw covered in stubble, and long black hair pulled back into a ponytail along the top of his head with the sides shaved. His green eyes twinkled as he caught me staring at him. His smile widened and he gave me a wink.

I rolled my eyes and turned my attention to the candidates already walking across the stage.

All had gotten offers so far.

"Nervous?" someone asked behind me.

I turned and the unfamiliar man stared straight at me. He was attractive, though not as much as the ones in front of me, slim, and had an aura about him that oozed positivity.

"Me?" I asked.

He smiled, showing off dimples. "Yeah."

"Not really," I replied.

He arched a brow. "Already have a guild picked?"

I shook my head. It was common for the richer families to pay their way into guilds. I laughed bitterly. "No."

He canted his head as he looked at me. "Yet, you aren't nervous?"

I had to move forward as the line moved up and caught two of the three in front of me eavesdropping.

These two were smaller than the first, but still larger than me. One had short red hair that curled at the ends, bright green eyes that shone with interest, and a pointed nose that reminded me of Loki. The other had pale blonde hair with a few streaks of red, a square jaw that looked like it might hurt to punch, and a slightly upturned nose. He reminded me of someone, but I couldn't put my finger on who.

"No," I replied without turning around. "It is unlikely that I will get drafted."

"Do you have a guild that you want to join?" he asked.

I looked up at the guild masters sitting in box seats over the crowd. Each box had their guild's banner flying from it. At the far side was a small guild. They were made up of misfits and took on the crazier jobs, but over the years I had seen them and seen the friendships blossoming among them. They were a family.

That was what I wanted. A true family.

"Yes," I said softly.

The three before me and the one behind me all wore equally curious expressions.

I ignored them.

Each of the three boys who had stood in front of me tested with high levels of magic and multiple guilds made offers.

Surprisingly, they all chose the Scarlet Dragons, the guild I wanted to join.

"Good luck," the guy behind me said in a low voice.

"You, too."

Taking a breath, I walked up the stairs and to the proctor who held the magic scanner, a black box with a display for the magic level.

He was in his forties, wore black glasses he had to keep pushing up his thin nose, and looked bored. "Hold out your arm," he instructed in a monotone voice.

With my eyes averted, I raised my arm.

He pressed the scanner to my skin and the audience quieted.

The scanner beeped and no one spoke.

"That can't be right," the proctor said.

I looked up and stared at my high score.

I'd seen my score once before, when I'd stolen our town's scanner and gone off into the forest to test it, but this score ...

This score was even higher.

Nice, I leveled up.

That thought was short lived as he pressed the scanner to my arm again and it gave the same result. My true power shouldn't have been detected when I wasn't using my magic, when it was securely bottled up.

The audience erupted.

And the guild masters raised their hands.

All of them, but Scarlet Dragon.

I stared at the Scarlet Dragon guild master, silently begging him to raise his hand.

The three guys who had been in front of me were standing on each side of the guild master, talking to him, but he didn't move.

"Choose," the proctor said.

I looked over at the guilds with their hands raised. The second on my list, the Golden Alicorn, had their hand raised. They were a larger guild and looked like they were decent. No awful rumors were circling about them either.

"Golden Alicorn," I said.

The crowd cheered.

I took one last look at the Scarlet Dragon guild, the three green-eyed guys who were still staring at me, and walked off the stage to join my new guild.

It was disappointing, but being able to join a guild at all was a great thing.

At the bottom of the stairs stood a tall man with deep set, dark eyes, shaved head, and a thick neck. Everyone knew him because he was one of the most powerful fighters in the world.

Silas.

"Follow me," he said, turning away.

I followed, keeping my eyes down and tried to ignore all of the murmurs around me. Why had my true score been shown? Checking myself now, I could feel my magic was properly contained.

"Your score is incredibly high for an unknown woman of your age," Silas said while still walking.

"I'm from a small town," I said.

"How old are you?"

"Twenty."

He glanced at me over his shoulder. "Why are you joining a guild now?"

"I felt it was the right time," I answered vaguely.

"Tired of hiding in the shadows and starving?" he asked.

Most would have said those words snidely, but he said them with understanding.

"Maybe," I muttered.

"You have issues with any members here, come tell me, alright?" he whispered once we reached the door to the guild's room.

All new members would wait in the room until the draft was over, and then we would all be taken to our new home.

"Okay," I whispered back, unsure what he meant, but appreciative of the gesture anyway.

He nodded and opened the door, waving me in and then shut it once I entered.

Ten guys in their late teens looked up when I entered.

"Hi," I said, raising my hand.

"Was that really your score?" one of them asked. He was the youngest looking and seemed genuinely curious.

I shrugged. "That's what the scanner said. Twice. So, I guess it is."

"How?" another asked. "Your score was almost as high as Silas's."

I shrugged. "How is anyone's magic at any level? It just is. Or, they practice and work to increase it."

"So, which is it?" the oldest of the group asked.

"Both," I said and sat on an empty chair in a corner.

The guy who had been behind me in line walked inside and smiled at me. "Looks like you got picked up after all."

I chuckled. "Looks like it."

He sat beside me and set his crossed feet on the table before us.

"Who are you?" one of the guys asked.

The guy beside me said, "Dart."

"You know her, Dart?" the oldest guy asked, and I could smell his disdain for me from here.

Wonderful. I hadn't even gotten to the guild and one of the members disliked me.

Dart looked at me. "Her? She was in line in front of me. I don't even know your name. Wow, I'm a jerk." He held out his hand. "I'm Dart."

I shook his hand. "Nadia."

Dart looked back at the guy and said, "Yeah, I know her. Why?"

The guy scowled at us and turned away, watching the screen and the last few people being drafted.

"What'd you do, piss in his cereal?" Dart asked out of the side of his mouth.

I shrugged. "My existence apparently bothers him."

"Your score bothers me," the guy said through gritted teeth. "There's no way someone as pathetic looking as you has a score that high."

Silas pushed open the door and stood in the doorway with his arms folded and a bored expression on his face. "Care to find out?" he asked.

I blinked at Silas's question. Did he expect me to fight this guy?

"Yes," the guy said.

Silas smiled. "Once we get to the guild, we'll settle this."

"Uh, I don't want to fight him." The last thing I needed was to embarrass this guy and have an actual enemy and not just someone annoyed I had a higher score.

Silas looked at me and he just continued to smile.

Okay, then.

"Time to go," Silas ordered and pushed off the doorframe.

"I got your back," Dart assured me as we stood.

"Thanks," I smiled.

Sadly, I was probably going to need it.

2

We filed out and stood in line, waiting our turn to use the portals.

"So, what's your story?" one of the guys asked me.

I shrugged. "Not much of a story. From a small town on the outskirts of the territory."

"You're a poor kid, aren't you?" the rude guy asked with a smirk.

"Monetarily poor, but obviously not magically," I said with a sweet smile.

Dart let out a bark of laughter. "Should I call a healer for that burn?"

Silas cleared his throat and I saw him smile before he let it disappear. "We're up. Everyone, step through."

One at a time, we stepped through the portal. When we stepped out, my eyes widened and my jaw dropped.

I'd known Golden Alicorn was large, but I hadn't known they had three mansions at their headquarters.

"Dirt squirrel is in awe," the jerk said.

"Alright, time to settle this," Silas said, a growl in his voice.

I tensed. "He's an ass, but I don't want to fight him."

"Afraid?" the guy asked.

Silas pointed at a silver dome. "You two, inside. Anyone else who wants to watch and witness this, inside as well."

Everyone marched into the dome, which turned out to be a large fighting arena.

The guy shook out his hands and smiled smugly.

That smile disappeared when Silas faced him and said, "Your opponent is me."

"What?" the guy and I asked at the same time.

"You want to join this guild, yet the first thing you do is verbally attack a fellow member just because she's more powerful than you and your fragile ego can't take it. So, since she and I have similar levels, you can face me and if you win, you can stay. Or, you can apologize to her right now, and if she accepts, you can stay. If you lose or refuse to apologize, you can go right back through that portal."

"You're not the guild master," the jerk said and folded his arms across his chest. "You can't make those decisions."

"Yes, he can," Paolo, the guild master of the Golden Alicorns, said as he entered the dome. He was one of the most powerful men on the planet, exuding an air of authority that was countered by his barely five-foot stature and thin body. He had wide brown eyes, a hooked nose, and a cleft chin. "He's my second and can make any decision he feels appropriate."

I froze.

Crap.

Would he be mad that I was causing these problems?

"You can't be serious? She's just a poor girl. A nobody," he snapped.

"And you're just a spoiled rich brat with an average magic level," Paolo said. "Make your choice."

"Man, forget this. I'll go join the Silver Serpents. They have standards there," the jerk said, and left.

"Bye," Dart yelled and waved to him with a wide smile.

I snickered, but stopped quickly when Paolo turned to face me.

I bowed quickly. "I'm sorry to cause you trouble."

"You did nothing," Silas snapped.

"You looked as surprised by your magic level as everyone else in that arena. Why?" Paolo asked.

I glanced at the other guys and at then Silas and Dart. "Um …"

"Recruits, go into the main house and Taron will help you," Silas said.

Dart glanced at me and I gave him a tiny nod. He left with the others, leaving me alone with Silas and Paolo.

Silas arched a brow at me.

"Most scanners can't detect my magic because it's not … *normal*," I said.

"How?" Paolo asked.

"Do you sense my magic?" I asked.

Silas and Paolo shook their heads.

I closed my eyes. "Goddess, grant me my magic so I might join this guild to further our plans of domination," I whispered in my mind.

"Granted," a sultry voice whispered in response.

Within me, a valve opened and my power poured into me.

My head dropped back, a smile curved my lips, and I opened my eyes, looking at the two men before me. I held enough back so the wings wouldn't come out, but my rainbow hair glowed brighter still, casting a multitude of rainbows around the room. "How about now?" I asked, even though they could obviously see and sense my magic now.

"What is this?" Paolo asked. "How are you able to seal your magic so?"

"A demoness stole my magic when I was young. She sealed it within a magical container. In order to access it, I had to make a deal with her."

"What type of deal?" Silas asked.

Before I could answer, Paolo interrupted to recap what I'd explained. "So, your magic is concealed because she has it stored in an inter-dimensional container. And, for some reason, the magic scanner picked it up anyway."

I nodded.

"I knew you were a good choice." Paolo chuckled and smiled.

"Does she have the ability to control you?" Silas asked.

I shook my head. "I was smart enough to bargain that out."

He nodded. "Good."

"So, why didn't you want to fight that idiot?" Paolo asked.

I sighed and let my magic go back to the container. "Because I don't like hurting people who don't deserve it, and while he was a jerk, he didn't deserve to have me beat him up. Plus, if we were going to be part of the same guild, I didn't want to start our relationship off that way."

"Let's get to the house and show you to your room," Silas said.

"Thank you," I said and bowed to him.

He waited until I straightened to speak. "No need to thank me. We're guild members. Backing each other up is what we're supposed to do." He winked and then turned and opened the door for Paolo and I.

"How long is your contract with the demoness?" Paolo asked as we walked towards the mansion they considered their main house.

"Until I produce a child for her … or fifty years," I said. "So, fifty years because I refuse to produce a child for her."

"You intend to be childless for your life?" Silas asked.

I nodded.

"And single?" Paolo asked.

I shrugged. "Unless I find someone who doesn't want children."

"So, who was your first choice?" Paolo asked.

I looked at him and my cheeks warmed as dirty thoughts went through my mind. "Huh?"

"For a guild. I could tell it wasn't us."

I flinched. "I honestly didn't expect to get any offers, so I was really surprised with what happened. I had planned to approach Scarlet Dragon afterwards first, and then come here if they denied me."

"Would you rather go to their guild?" he asked.

I stopped walking and stared at him. "What?"

"I'm sure if Brandon heard you wanted to go to his guild that he would let you in," Paolo said.

"But he didn't raise his hand," I said. "You did."

He smiled. "I'm sure he had his reasons."

"Thank you, but I wouldn't feel right doing something like that," I said and resumed walking.

The fact that Silas had stuck up for me, and Paolo was willing to do something like that spoke volumes of their character and made me hope I could have a family here, too.

3

Dart waited in the foyer when we walked in. His quick glance over me warmed my heart.

He had been worried about me.

"Dart, we aren't that kind of guild," Silas huffed.

Dart smiled and put his hands in his pockets. "Didn't say anything, Silas."

"You know which room she's getting?" Paolo asked.

Dart nodded.

"Why don't you show her? Then, you two be sure to come down for dinner." Paolo turned and Silas gave me a smile before following after him. My traitorous body reacted to that smile. Why could just a smile from him make me hotter?

Dart turned towards a set of white marble stairs and I hurried to catch up.

"You okay?" he asked softly as we ascended side by side.

I nodded. "Thanks for worrying."

He glanced over his shoulder and smiled. "Guild members always look after each other."

I returned his smile and followed him down a long hallway lined with doors.

"They have the new recruits stay in the main house for their first year because it's often that they'll leave and go to a different guild, and it's easier to move them in and out of here. Or, at least, that's what they said." He stopped at one door and pushed it open. "This is your room. Mine is across the hall." He pointed behind him.

"Thanks," I said, stepping inside. The room was rather sparse; just a bed, dresser, and a lamp, but it was more than I had had at home and much bigger.

"Do you want to talk about what happened between you three?" he asked.

I smiled. "We just talked. Nothing happened."

He nodded. "I get it, you don't know me well enough to trust me with secrets yet. It's okay."

My brows furrowed. "That's not—"

"Where's your luggage?" he asked, interrupting me.

"I don't have any," I admitted.

His brows furrowed. "What about clothes?"

"My sister has them now."

"We should take a job as soon as we can," he said. "Come on, let's go down for dinner."

He changed the topics so fast I was dizzy.

I followed him and asked, "How do you even know where to go?"

"One of my talents," he said. "I can see heat signatures through walls."

My jaw dropped. "That's so cool."

He pushed open one of a set of double doors and sure enough, we had made it to the dining hall.

Hundreds of heads swiveled in our direction and silence greeted us.

Dart raised his hand and smiled wide. "Yo."

Marcus, a high-level fire wielder, stood and walked to stand before us, hands on his hips as he looked down at me.

I held my breath and tried to stop my shaking hands.

"You don't seem all that powerful," he said as he continued to look down his nose at me.

I shrugged. "Looks can be deceiving."

Not for the first time, I was glad for my snarky mouth.

He smirked. "True." He sidestepped and waved one arm to let us pass.

Dart headed to a half-full table and sat.

With nothing else to do, I followed him and sat on his left.

Dart had already started a discussion with the others at the table and was laughing with them.

Why couldn't I be like that? Why couldn't I be less shy? Once I knew someone, I had no problems, or if it was for work, but the first few interactions were always awkward.

Silas sat across from me and joined in with the conversation at the table.

He really was rather handsome. Why was he single? Someone as powerful and attractive as him likely had women flocking to him. Perhaps he didn't like women? Or maybe he just wanted to focus on increasing his power first?

A short time later, Paolo entered and food was served. Normally, we would get our food from the line, but since it was a special day, they served us at the tables.

The conversations didn't waver despite the food, but I stayed silent as I ate.

Paolo stood and clapped twice to get our attention. "We have new members, as you're aware. And it is time for them to officially join our guild. New members, please come up here."

Dart and I stood and walked to Paolo, along with the other three new members.

"This mark is more than a mark. It links us all together. Our powers are combined, as are our heartbeats. If one of us is in grave danger, it will alert everyone else. We are not just a guild, but a team, a family. We look out for each other and we do our best to uphold the values of the guild. Each and every one of you represents Golden Alicorn. Don't forget that." He pulled a wand from his pocket and smiled wide. "Who's first?"

Dart stepped forward with his forearm out and Paolo pressed the wand to his skin. A golden alicorn appeared and all the gathered members shuddered as his joining affected them.

The others took their turns, each getting the mark in a different spot.

Being last had given me time to decide where I wanted the mark. I stepped up and pulled my shirt down to the side, exposing my shoulder blade.

Paolo pressed the wand to my skin and for a brief second, pain seared through my shoulder, but then disappeared.

Marcus stood. "What was that? I thought she was powerful."

Several others murmured and most scowled.

Paolo raised his hand and everyone quieted. "Her magic is hidden until she needs it. Silas and I both witnessed it."

"I don't buy it," Marcus growled.

Silas stood and smiled, but there was nothing kind in the smile. "Did you just call your guild master and me a liar?"

Marcus continued his glare.

"I can prove it," I said.

"You don't have to," Paolo said.

I smiled. "You're all my family, right? I can show them I truly have the power."

I prepared to do it, but the doors being kicked open distracted me.

Zachary, a man in his thirties with a thick beard and dark eyes who could manipulate earth, walked in with a huge grin. "Why didn't anyone tell me we had new members?"

Paolo sighed softly. "Zachary, we do this every year."

Zachary walked up to me and held out his hand.

I shook it and returned his smile.

"Name's Zachary. Who are you?"

"I'm…"

He moved to Dart without waiting for my answer.

"… Nadia." I finished the answer in a whisper since he had moved on.

Paolo leaned over and whispered, "He's a bit crazy, forgive him."

I shrugged. "He seems nice."

"Why aren't we celebrating? Why does everyone look so serious?" Zachary asked. He slapped his hands on the shoulders of the other new members. "Let's drink!"

"Paolo, can we look at the bulletin boards?" Dart asked.

Paolo frowned, taken aback by the request. "Yes, but for your first mission, you need to take an existing member with you."

"Okay," Dart said. "Can we do that in a trio? Nadia and I were hoping to work together."

Silas walked up. "I'll join them."

My eyes widened a moment and then narrowed in suspicion.

Was he trying to keep tabs on me because of what I'd shared with them?

"Wouldn't be the first man to have his doubts about you," Norma said.

Dart smiled and said, "Great."

His comment pulled me out of my head and my attention away from Norma.

Silas led the way and Dart and I followed.

Adjacent to the dining hall was a room lined with cork-boards with a dozen or more notecard sized pieces of paper tacked to them. Each notecard was a mission. At the top of the board was a number from one to ten to indicate the approximate difficulty level of a job.

I expected us to start with a second level job since we were newbies, but Silas surprised me by walking to the fifth level board. He turned to us and tilted his head towards the board. "Pick one."

Dart stepped up and began reading the various notes.

I stepped closer to Silas. "Why?" I asked. "Are you unconvinced or still untrusting of me?"

Silas scowled. "You don't trust easily, do you?"

My cheeks heated. "Where I'm from, people don't do

things without a reason, usually involving money or power."

"How about this one, Nadia?" Dart asked.

I stepped away from Silas and walked to Dart, reading the job. It seemed simple enough, fight some bandits trying to take over a small town.

"This looks good," I said.

Silas peered over my shoulder. "Agreed." He grabbed the note and tapped the little checkmark at the bottom of the paper. A green puff of magic smoke popped up from the note at the same time a golden band formed around all three of our wrists. Within a second the note disintegrated.

"This is going to be super fun," Dart said, beaming and practically wiggling with excitement like a puppy.

Silas returned his smile. "It will definitely be a great learning experience." His glance in my direction had my hackles up. He was definitely hiding something.

"Leave first thing tomorrow?" Dart asked.

Silas nodded.

I spun away. "Great, I'll see you tomorrow."

4

Silas, Dart, and I walked into town, headed for the portal center.

I was so busy looking at the vendors that I ran into the trio of guys from the draft, literally.

"Hello," the shortest one said as he held my arm, keeping me upright after bouncing off his chest. He had short, red hair that curled at the ends despite how short it was. It made me wonder how curly it would be if he let it grow out.

I smiled. "Sorry, I wasn't watching where I was going."

My eye caught on his Scarlet Dragon mark and my smile wilted.

"I'm Grayson," he said and held out his hand. "They're Jasper and Parker."

I shook his hand. "I'm—"

"Nadia," Dart called as he and Silas backtracked to me.

Silas glared at the trio. "Everything alright?" he asked me.

Grayson continued to smile. "Just saying hi." He winked at me. "Hope to bump into you again soon, Nadia."

"Same," I said as I watched them leave.

"Come on," Silas urged.

I followed my step a little peppier. They sure were nice on the eyes.

"*Yes, they are,*" Norma purred.

"*Dibs,*" I teased back mentally.

"Those were the guys who were in front of us at the drafts, right?" Dart asked.

I nodded.

"You know them?"

I shook my head.

He scowled. "Huh."

Unsure what to say, I stayed quiet. A few steps later, I put my hand in my pocket and pulled out a folded piece of paper.

Turning my back so Silas and Dart wouldn't see, I opened it. The note only had three lines and three signatures.

We're sorry you didn't get into Scarlet Dragon.
We'd like to get to know you better.
Summon us with a drop of blood over our signatures.
Grayson Jasper Parker

When had they slipped that in my pocket? When had they written it? Had they planned to find me or had they kept it with them on the off chance they would eventually see me?

I folded it back up and put it in my pocket.

What crafty boys. I was definitely going to meet up with them again.

As usual, the portal center was packed, so we got into line to wait for our turn. It seemed like I was always waiting. Waiting to get into the portals. Waiting to get into the guild. Waiting to find someone who might be interested in me despite my demon problem.

"So, what's the plan?" Dart asked Silas. He flipped a coin between his knuckles without focusing on it, leading me to believe it was something he often did when bored.

"We'll scope things out first and then make our plan of action," he growled.

"Why are you mad?" I asked. He'd been almost cheery this morning.

He rubbed his face. "I'm not. Just didn't sleep well."

"*Liar*," Norma whispered in my head.

I almost rolled my eyes. I didn't need a demon to know he was lying.

Dart looked at me with a quirked brow and I shrugged.

It took an hour before it was our turn to use the portals, time I used to consider any issues that might arise on my first mission and how to combat them. Although many thought it pessimistic, I preferred to think of the worst possible situations that might arise, so I could figure out a solution to them beforehand. That way, if it happened, I was prepared and not caught off guard.

Silas paid and the portal employee activated it for us.

The middle-aged man looked incredibly bored as he took money, activated portals, and waved people through. His clothes were really nice, so at least the job paid well.

Dart saluted the employee and walked through the portal with a big smile.

The employee gave no reaction.

"You next," Silas said.

I opened my mouth to argue, when my father's deep voice yelled out my name.

Everyone turned to look at him. His cheeks were red, eyes bloodshot, and I could smell the alcohol even from so far away. "Nadia, come here," he snapped.

Trembling, I backed up towards the portal.

"Nadia?" Silas asked softly while keeping his eyes on my dad.

Dad pulled his whip from his belt and his magic crackled down it. Terror swept through me at the sight of it. I jumped through the portal and collided with Dart on the other side.

He caught me and somehow didn't fall over. "Nadia, what's wrong?"

I jerked free from him and backed away; eyes fixed on the portal.

Silas stepped through, looked around until he saw me, and walked straight for me.

I held my ground, eyes fixed on the portal. Waiting. Terrified. Unable to breathe.

The magic swirling within the circle finally disappeared.

"Nadia!" Silas yelled in my face.

I jumped back, a dagger in my hand.

Dart and Silas looked at the dagger and me.

"Come on," I said and spun away, putting the dagger away so I didn't accidentally stab someone.

The farther we got from the portal, the better.

"Who was that?" Silas asked.

"What?" Dart asked, looking between us.

I walked faster. "My dad."

Silas grabbed my wrist and jerked me back, keeping me from getting run over by a horse drawn cart that thundered down the road.

I rubbed my face and shoved all my emotions into the box they belonged in. "Thanks."

"That was your dad?" Silas asked.

I nodded.

"He's hurt you?" he asked.

Images started to escape the box, but I slammed the mental lid closed.

"Yeah." There was no point in lying.

"Your dad hurt you?" Dart asked.

I nodded and then turned and smiled at them. "It's okay. I'm with you guys now, so what happened before doesn't matter."

"*Liar*," Norma sung.

Fucking Norma.

Silas looked back at the portal like he was debating returning to confront my dad.

"Come on," I urged. "We've got a ways to walk before we can start our recon."

Silas followed me and Dart walked at his side, whispering to him.

Dammit. Why had that jerk been there? Was he

tracking me?

I looked down at my arm and the rough scar. He had implanted a device in my arm, but I had removed it. Had I not gotten it all?

Or were there more?

"*There are no more trackers,*" Norma said.

"You sure?" I whispered.

"*Yes,*" she replied immediately.

"What?" Dart asked.

I resumed walking. "Nothing."

Silas led us to a hill that overlooked the town with a bandit problem.

We lay down on the grass and nibbled on some dried meat while we watched, waiting for the bandits to show.

Silas reached over Dart's back to hand me the water, since Dart lay between us. He caught my hand as I grabbed the water. "You and I need to talk when we return."

I jerked free of his hold and didn't respond, focused back on the town.

It was small, maybe thirty people total, and all of the townspeople wore dirty, stained, and patched clothes.

It reminded me of the town I had grown up in.

As darkness fell, lanterns lit up with magic inside of the houses and out front of a few. Within minutes, the bandits appeared.

There was at least a dozen of them, all armed with swords, and four or so flaunting fire magic. All of them wore smug expressions, laughing and bantering with each other as they headed to cause trouble.

I stood, but Silas held out a hand. "Wait," he ordered me.

"Wait? For them to hurt someone? No."

Dart grabbed my hand. "We're outnumbered. We need to see what we're up against first."

I stayed despite hating it, because he was right.

The bandits knocked over some fruit stands and then surrounded an older man. Before I even inhaled, one of them punched the old man and knocked him to the ground. The other bandits laughed, throwing their heads back as though it were the funniest thing they had ever seen.

My body moved, my powers activated, and I ran right in between them, putting myself in front of the old man. "Knock it off," I snapped.

The men looked me over with sneers.

The one who had punched the older man spoke, clearly the leader. "Who are you? I haven't seen you in town before."

"Get out of this town and leave these people alone," I snapped. "This is your final warning."

Magic coursed through me, but not my full amount, just enough to kick their butts. Norma was surprisingly good at knowing how much power I would need.

One of the bandits smiled, showing me broken brown teeth. "I think instead, we'll have some fun with you."

He reached towards me, his fingernails broken and his hand covered in dirt.

I punched him in the face as hard as I could. Bone crunched, blood sprayed, and he howled in pain.

"Run," I urged the old man.

He didn't hesitate, scurrying away while the bandits focused on me.

"You're going to pay for that," the bleeding bandit

growled.

"Well, I don't have any money, so you'll have to put it on a tab," I said and winked at him.

"Get her!"

The guys nearest him, who had up until that point just stared in disbelief, charged forward. I managed to duck one punch and block another, but the third caught me in the stomach. The air whooshed out of my lungs and forced a momentary pause in my reaction.

Two more guys ran over and grabbed my arms, holding me so they could take turns punching me.

Unfortunately, they didn't know I hadn't come alone.

The guys holding my arms were suddenly airborne and screaming.

I launched forward, kicked one guy in the stomach and knocked his legs out from under him.

Dart lived up to his name, darting between each of the guys, stabbing them in spots that hurt, but wouldn't kill them.

Silas walked into the town; his eyes glowed as he held aloft the guys who had held me by his magic alone. "You really need to learn how to properly treat women."

"Who are you?" the bleeding bandit asked.

"That's Silas," one of the floating men gasped. "From the Golden Alicorn Guild."

"Oh, crap," one of the others said.

"Leave this place and never return," Silas said. "If you come back, I won't be merciful."

He released his magic and the men fell to the ground, making multiple thuds and groans. Quickly, they helped each other up and ran out of the town.

"What were you thinking?" Silas growled as he stalked over to me. "If we hadn't been here, you could have—"

"Thank you," the old man said as he hobbled back over to me. "If you hadn't stopped them, they probably would have killed me this time." He bowed to me, reached up, and kissed the back of my hand. "Thank you."

Silas and I watched him hobble inside of a house and an old woman hugged him with tears in her eyes.

"I couldn't let them hurt him," I said softly to Silas. "I would rather trade myself and endure the pain than to watch them hurt someone else."

"They're retreating," Dart said as he came back to us. He walked over and examined my face. "You're going to have a few bruises, but you seem fine otherwise."

I smiled. "I'm fine."

"We're going to stay here tonight," Silas said to the old man. "We want to make sure they don't come back for retaliation, which they likely will."

A woman in her forties with long, silver hair walked over to us. "You can stay in my home. I have spare rooms. The bandits like to return after midnight, so we should get you food and rest until then."

"Thank you," Silas said and smiled warmly at her.

For some reason, anger coursed through my body.

"That's called jealousy," Norma laughed in my head.

No. There was no reason for me to be jealous. I didn't even know him.

Dart and I followed behind Silas and the woman, and I kept my eyes on the ground. Whatever these feelings were, they could go in the box with all the rest. They would not help me in my goals and as such, were useless.

We returned to the guild the following day, after we'd ensured the bandits had left the region.

As he'd predicted, I had quite a nice black eye from one of the punches I'd received, but saving the man had been worth it.

Silas hadn't spoken to me since yelling at me, and I found I was okay with it. The less I talked with him, the better.

As we walked towards the front door of the main mansion of The Golden Alicorns, the sky filled with clouds, lightning and thunder booming and crackling.

I sighed and let my head drop forward as rain began to pour from the clouds. "Dammit."

Silas and Dart hurried beneath the porch, but I stayed in the open.

"Get in here or you'll get soaked," Dart yelled.

I held out my arms. "You see any wet spots?"

Silas and he scowled.

"Why aren't you getting wet?" Silas asked.

"Because he isn't allowed to get me wet," I said and pointed up at the glowing figure descending from the clouds.

Their eyes widened.

"You're bruised. Who did it? Where are they? I'll crush their skulls in," Thor, God of Thunder, said as he came to stand beside me, his hammer, Mjolnir in his hand.

"We took care of it. Why are you here?" I asked, turning to face him with hands on my hips.

"It's time," he said.

I cringed. "I'm sorry. I forgot."

His brows furrowed. "You forgot about your date with a god?"

"Wait, you're dating Thor?" Silas asked.

"No," I said and shook my head. "He and I are just friends."

"Only because you don't want to help me spawn demigods," Thor muttered.

I glared at him. "I'm not a broodmare."

He glared back. "I never said you were. Besides, would sleeping with me be so bad?"

I looked up at the sky. "Odin, help me. I am not answering that."

"You know a god and you still can't get rid of the demon?" Silas asked.

"Demon? What demon?" Thor asked.

I groaned. "Shut up, Silas."

The air sizzled and thunder boomed overhead. "Nadia."

I snapped my fingers. "Invisible."

Thor glared at me. "I am not—"

"Rules!" I yelled and stamped my foot.

"Rule six point two, this involves your safety and super-sedes all other rules," Thor said.

"You don't know that," I countered and folded my arms over my chest.

"You there, what is the demon problem?" Thor asked and pointed Mjolnir at Silas.

"Shut up, Silas!" I yelled.

"You know a god and your dad is still alive?" Dart asked.

These two men were going to be the death of me!

"What?" Thor asked. "What are they talking about?"

"You've kept all of your worst issues a secret from him, why?" Dart asked.

"Nadia, what are they talking about?" Thor asked me.

Thor could have saved me from my father, but the two times I had tried to summon him, he hadn't come. I'd thought he had abandoned me, but later learned he had been on another planet fighting a battle. I hadn't wanted to tell him the truth after he returned.

"Her father abused her and she is under a contract with a demon," Silas said.

Memories of the pain and sadness at being alone and abused surfaced and my chest tightened, making it hard to breathe.

Silas and Dart looked at me, their faces pinched. Then, almost the entire guild ran out of the mansions and out to us.

Thor gripped Mjolnir tight, glaring down at me with lightning in his eyes. "Tell me they're lying," he whispered.

I clutched at the front of my shirt, willing the pain to go away, to go back in the box it belonged in.

"What is this pain?" Paolo asked. "What is going on?"

"Is that Thor?" Marcus asked.

Thor reached out towards me, but I smacked his hand away. Rage consumed me, allowing me to swallow the pain and shove it back into the box it lived in. Norma let loose almost half of my powers and my body began to glow and float, my rainbow hair casting colors that bounced off the buildings and ground.

"Do not touch me, Thunderer," I growled, my voice resonated with dark energy and echoed around the courtyard.

"Nadia, you tell me the truth right now," he ordered me, glowing himself with lightning crackling along Mjolnir.

"She's going to fight a god?" Marcus gaped.

"I will shove Mjolnir up your ass if you don't back down," I snapped. The ground began to rumble in the spot my feet had been and pieces of it floated up around me.

Thor's eyes filled with lightning until they were solid white, but after taking a deep breath, he set Mjolnir down, released his powers, and opened his arms.

Instantly, the rage disappeared and my magic with it. I ran into his arms and let him hug me.

"My friend, my little ivy, you must tell me what has happened," he whispered in my ear.

"Why can we feel her emotional pain like it is physical?" Silas asked Paolo.

Paolo whispered, "I don't know."

"Not in front of them," I whispered into Thor's chest. I couldn't cry in front of them.

Thor picked up Mjolnir, wrapped his arms tighter

around me, and then we soared across the rainbow bridge to Asgard.

When I opened my eyes, we stood inside Thor's house. Most assumed his house would be timber beams, wooden floors, and such. That was completely wrong. He loved shiny things, something I teased him about often. The house was made of polished, white granite, the floors and counters obsidian with glittery stardust, and his tables made of smoky quartz.

He released me and sat in one of his chairs, a fluffy monstrosity that felt like being hugged by a cloud. "Speak," he ordered me.

"Dad abused me. I didn't tell you because you were off-world when it started happening with increasing frequency. You were fighting in a war. I ended up being forced into a deal with a demon. She has control of my magic. I have to either provide her a child, or deal with her for fifty years. So, I'm dealing with her for fifty years."

"What else is she making you do?" he asked, narrowing his eyes.

"Becoming as strong as I can," I said with a shrug.

"Why didn't you come to me?" he asked.

"I tried to call you when he started hurting me, but you couldn't hear me since you were so far away," I said, my voice becoming quieter the more I spoke.

"What are you hiding about the demon? If I can get the container, I'm sure I can open it."

I shook my head. "It is sealed with runes."

His eyes widened. "Can you show me?"

I sighed. "Yeah."

He walked to me, pressed his forehead to mine, and I pictured the container and the runes.

After a moment, he pulled away and paced across the room. "That is very old magic. Father might be able to break it, but—"

"We are not involving Odin," I said quickly. "I will bear with it. I made the deal and I will endure the consequences."

"Is that the guild you wanted to join?" he asked.

I shook my head. "The one I wanted did not raise their hand. This guild did and they're good so far."

"I'll keep an eye on them. Is there anything else you need to tell me?"

I shook my head and sat in one of the chairs. "What's new with you?"

He scoffed. "Nothing."

With a sigh, I said, "You should probably return me. They're probably worried. Or think I'm screwing you."

"Which is apparently a horrible thing," he muttered.

I rolled my eyes. "Come on."

"Next time you need me, call until I come, okay?" he whispered as he hugged me. "I'm sorry I wasn't there for you when you needed me."

Tears escaped and I cried into his chest. "I was so scared. I thought you abandoned me."

He squeezed me. "I will never abandon you."

As soon as my tears were spent, we returned to the guild and found Silas still outside.

"This one interests me," Thor whispered.

"You okay?" Silas asked.

"And if she wasn't, would you fight me for her honor?" Thor asked Silas.

Silas's jaw clenched. "Why are you meddling with a mortal?"

"Why do you care?" Thor asked. "She is not yours and you are not hers."

"Thor," I snapped, "stop goading him. Silas, I'm fine. Thor and I are friends."

"Friends, huh?" Marcus asked from an open window.

Thor glared at Marcus. "I do not like this one."

Marcus's eyes widened and he smartly took a step back.

"It's not wise to provoke a god," I whispered to him. "I only do it with Thor because we have a contract that states he cannot hurt me."

"Among other things," Thor mumbled.

"You're the idiot that signed the contract," I reminded him with hands on my hips and an eyebrow arched.

"I didn't realize a seven-year-old would be so crafty," he grumbled.

"You should have read it," I said and smiled wide.

"Yeah. Yeah. I'm going to leave you to your guild. You, Silas, protect her or you'll answer to me," Thor said.

"He isn't my partner," I said, but Thor had already disappeared in a flash of lightning.

I groaned and walked into the mansion. Silas followed me, silently, until we were at my bedroom door.

"Are you really alright?" he asked.

I nodded. "Yes. Thor and I are really just friends."

"Are you mad at me?" he asked.

I turned and smiled at him. "You told on me to Thor, so yeah, I'm mad. However, it worked out, so I guess I'll let it slide this once. But you still haven't apologized for yelling at me, so I'm still mad about that."

He scowled. "Yelling at you? What? Two days ago? About running into danger? Why would I apologize about that? You were reckless and could have died."

"No, that man would have died if I hadn't run in. I saved his life in exchange for some bruises. We are supposed to protect those weaker than us. What's the point of being in a guild if we aren't going to save people?"

He opened his mouth and then closed it.

"I need a nap. So, you'll have to excuse me," I said and shut my bedroom door behind me, locked it, and leaned against it with a sigh. Hopefully, this wasn't a precursor to how my life with the guild would be.

"*You could just sleep with Silas and get it out of your systems,*" Norma whispered.

"Shut up," I growled back.

Fucking Norma.

The nap evaded me and I gave up a half hour later. With a sigh, I showered and then went to the dining hall.

6

There was a surprising number of members at the dining hall, and all stared at me when I entered.

Great. Thor just had to show up and make a scene.

Okay, I had been the one making a scene, but still.

Telling people stuff always ended up bad, but I was just a very honest person … most of the time. I worried Thor would tell Odin and they'd try to intervene with me and Norma.

Not that I wanted the demon holding my powers, but I didn't want to risk her taking them completely.

After getting some food, I sat at an empty table and started eating.

Paolo sat across from me. "So, you know gods. Is there anything else important I should know about you?"

I tapped my lips. "Thor and I have a contract and part of it is that I have to meet him once a month. He's very protective of me. Loki and I are … frenemies. He won't kill me, but he might push me in front of a spell he knows will hurt a lot. I was abused by my dad and he tried to confront me when we were leaving for our mission at the portal center. He'll probably try to hurt me if given the chance and is probably looking for me now. I call the demon Norma, and sometimes I talk to her out loud instead of in my head. I don't have any money or possessions because my family was poor. I left my clothes for my younger sister since Dad won't buy her new ones. I have a temper, as you saw when I got mad at Thor. Um … oh, Hel hates me. Yep, that's it."

Paolo stared at me with wide eyes.

"How did you meet the gods?" Silas asked as he sat next to Paolo.

I shoved the last bites of food in my mouth and stood without a word, headed towards the exit.

"Nadia," Silas called.

I ignored him and walked out of the room.

And right into Dart.

He smiled down at me. "Hey, what's your hurry?"

"Need some air," I said and spun around him and towards the door.

I pushed open the front door and walked out to the grassy area in front of it. I closed my eyes and breathed in deep. Sometimes, I got a little claustrophobic inside houses and needed to breathe the fresh air, to remind myself I wasn't trapped in a room my dad had locked anymore.

I shouldn't have been mad at Silas, yet seeing him had irked me. Why?

"*Because you want to sleep with him,*" Norma said.

"You okay?" Dart asked.

"You and I are going to be partners, right?" I asked with my eyes still closed.

"That was my plan," Dart said.

"Then you should know that one of things my dad did was lock me in my room for weeks at a time. So, sometimes I need to get outside of a building and breathe the fresh air. To remind myself I'm free."

"Why are you mad at Silas?"

"He yelled at me and hasn't apologized." I scowled. "And I don't know, something about him is making me angry."

"That's hardly fair," Dart said.

I sighed. "I know." I opened my eyes and faced him. "I'll try to stop it."

"I'm not a real affectionate person, I mean I touch people a lot in a friendly way, but if you ever need a hug, I'm willing to break that," Dart said with pink staining his cheeks as he kicked the dirt with the toe of his boot.

I smiled and gave him a quick hug. "Thanks, partner."

He smiled back. "Tomorrow, will you go shopping with me?"

"Sure."

He draped his arm over my shoulders and steered me back towards the house. "Come sit with me while I eat."

I sighed. "You're just trying to force me to interact with Silas."

"Why would I do that?" he asked with a wide smile.

"I don't know." I narrowed my eyes. "Why would you?"

He pushed open the door. "Who knows?"

"You do," I said and shook my head.

He laughed, and when we got to the table with Paolo and Silas, he pushed me down beside Silas.

"I'm sorry," I whispered to Silas. "That was rude of me."

"Can I talk to you for a second?" he asked.

Paolo watched us with a smirk.

Why was he smirking?

"Sure," I agreed and stood.

Silas led me out of the dining room and to an office two doors down. He closed the door behind him and said, "I'm sorry for yelling at you during our mission. I yelled because you'd scared me and I'd worried they were going to hurt you."

"I accept your apology," I said with a wide smile.

"I need you to be honest with me," he said. "Let me know when you're going to do something crazy like that."

My smile slipped. "I'm partners with Dart. I doubt we'll be working together anytime soon."

"We'll see," he said and shrugged.

"Why were you so aggressive to the trio from the other guild?" I asked.

He looked down. "I thought they might be trying to convince you to join their guild."

"No," I said. "I'm not leaving this guild unless something awful happens here."

"Like what?" he asked and raised his head.

I shrugged. "I don't know. I'm just saying I'm not going to leave easily."

"I'll make sure nothing happens," he said.

"I don't need a protector," I said. Despite my statement, warmth blossomed in my chest.

"How about a friend?" he asked and smiled.

Friend? Was that what he wanted to be?

I smiled. "I could always use more friends."

He nodded, opened the door, and we walked back to

the dining hall. Dart had his food and was talking with Paolo while he ate.

Silas and I sat down.

It was still my first week here and yet I'd made two friends. Two friends who seemed to truly care about me.

"Want to come into town with us tomorrow?" Dart asked Silas. "We're going to do some shopping."

"You're doing some shopping," I corrected.

Dart shook his head. "We got paid, so you're going to get some new clothes."

"I'm not spending my money on clothes," I said and rolled my eyes. "This outfit is fine."

"You can't wear the same outfit every day," Paolo said.

"Why not?" I asked. "I wash it."

"At least get one more outfit," Paolo said and smiled. "You can get clothes pretty cheap in town."

I frowned. "Fine. I'll get one more outfit."

"I've never met a girl who didn't like shopping," Dart said.

"Oh, I love shopping," I said. "I just hate spending money."

"Your trio seemed to work pretty well," Paolo commented.

Dart nodded. "It was nice having a third on the mission."

"What do you think about permanently having a third?" Paolo asked and looked at me.

I narrowed my eyes at Silas, but he was busy picking dirt from his fingernails.

"What about Silas's partner?" I asked.

Silas looked up and smiled. "I've never had a partner."

"Well, that settles it. You three will be our first trio. I'm going to implement trios with the other new members, too," Paolo said and stood. "Have a good night."

I looked back at Silas who was beaming like a dog who'd been given a bone.

"You realize you're going to have to deal with my craziness for as long as we're in a trio, right?" I asked him.

He shrugged. "Works for me. Plus, I'd rather be near you to keep you safe, so Thor doesn't come after me if you get hurt."

I rolled my eyes. "If it's my own fault, he won't hunt you down."

"We'll leave after breakfast tomorrow, okay?" Dart said. "I want to get to the stores before they get too crowded."

"What are you shopping for?" I asked.

He smiled. "That's a secret."

I rolled my eyes. "Okay."

7

The town was already bustling with activity as we walked down the streets, but the shops Dart went into were relatively empty. I stood outside with Silas, watching the people walking around.

A trio of familiar faces walked down the street.

I raised my hand and they raised theirs in return. They walked in my direction, so I met them halfway in the middle of the road.

"Hey, what are you boys up to?" I asked.

"We're doing a little shopping," Jasper said. His voice was a lot deeper than I'd thought it was going to be.

"You go on a mission yet?" Grayson asked.

I nodded. "How about you?"

They nodded.

Parker looked at Silas, who was glaring at them from his spot next to the shop's door. "Your boyfriend is mad you're talking to us."

"He's not my boyfriend," I said. "I'm single. He's one of my partners."

"What are you doing tonight?" Grayson asked. "Would you like to go to dinner with us?"

"I'd—"

"Nadia," Silas called.

I looked over at him with a scowl. "What?"

Dart stood beside him with a new bag. "Ready to go get some clothes?" Dart asked.

"Meet us at the port I at six o'clock," Parker whispered in my ear.

He smelled like cherries.

"Okay," I agreed.

All three smiled as they turned to walk away. They raised their hands to me and I raised mine to them in goodbye.

"I think they're stalking you," Dart teased.

I rolled my eyes. "They are not. Just because they're shopping, too, doesn't mean they're stalking me."

"So, what did they want?" Silas asked.

"Where are we going to get clothes from?" I asked Dart, headed towards the next set of buildings. "Hopefully, they have some discount racks."

"Over here," Dart said.

I followed behind him, ignoring the scowling Silas. He could be angry I was talking to guys from another guild all he wanted. I wasn't going to leave our guild, so he had nothing to worry about.

"What size are you?" Dart asked as we entered a clothing store.

"Small," I said, picking up the price tag on the nearest shirt. I almost fainted at the high number. "This probably isn't the place for me."

Dart browsed through clothes, pulling a few shirts and pants out. "Nonsense. Try these on."

I walked to the curtained area where patrons could try on the clothes, and tried them all on. "They fit," I called out as I changed back into my clothes.

"You're supposed to show us," Dart said with a chuckle.

I stepped out with the clothes in hand. "Why would I show you they fit?"

Silas looked up at the ceiling with a smile, like he was trying not to laugh.

"I don't understand," I whispered, feeling like an idiot for missing whatever they were saying, my cheeks hot with embarrassment.

"It's fine," Dart said and took the clothes. "These all fit?"

I nodded. "But they're too expensive." I said it quiet enough that the store owner wouldn't hear.

"That's not a problem," Silas said as he stood.

I snatched the clothes from Dart. "You are not buying me clothes."

"You need to buy clothes," Dart said. "Just let us help you. We're partners, remember?"

"I don't need this many," I said and separated out just another shirt and pair of pants.

Silas took all the clothes from me and marched to the counter.

"Silas," I gasped.

Dart grabbed a few other things and set them on the pile, too. "Just accept it, Nadia."

"No," I growled. "I'll pay you guys back when we do our next job."

"No, you won't," Silas said.

The shop owner put the clothes in a bag and handed it to Silas with a smile. "Thanks for your business."

"This is ridiculous," I grumbled. "You won't let me pay you back? Why not?"

"It's a gift," Dart said. "Accept it."

"But …" I hadn't been given a gift before.

"Nadia?" Silas asked.

I looked up at them with tears in my eyes. "No one has given me a gift before. Just let me pay you back."

"*You are a weepy mess today,*" Norma said with a chuckle.

"*Shut up, Norma,*" I growled in my head.

"What if we allow you pay us back for part of it?" Dart asked.

I nodded and turned away so I could wipe my face. "Okay."

"See, compromising is easy," Dart said and draped his arm over my shoulders again. "Come on, there's one more place I want to go."

I let him lead me out of the store, feeling a whole lot of emotions I hadn't before. Silas walked behind us, silent, and yet I felt like his mind was moving a mile a minute. If he were a machine, I was certain smoke would be billowing out of his ears. What was he thinking about?

We started by a shop with beautiful dresses and I stopped to admire them.

Dart walked backwards to come to me and Silas stopped on my other side.

"Someday, after I've gotten rid of Norma and can retire from the guild, I want to wear one of these," I said softly.

"Why wait until then?" Silas asked.

"Because then will be when I can finally marry a man," I said.

"You know, they do have balls and things you could wear a dress like that to," Dart said.

I rolled my eyes. "Like I would ever be invited to a ball."

"Yes, who would invite you to a ball?" Dad asked. "Unless it was to wipe up the floors."

I turned slowly and my eyes widened. He stood behind me, his whip out and magic running through it.

"You aren't running away from me this time, girl," he snapped. "You made a fool of me in front of everyone with your stunt on the stage."

"I didn't do anything," I said.

"Your magic. Did the demon open your magic up?" he asked.

I shook my head. "The reader was able to detect it somehow. She and I didn't do anything."

His whip cracked as he snapped it towards my throat, but Silas stuck his arm out and the whip wrapped around his forearm instead.

"You have thirty seconds to get out of my sight before I kill you," Silas said.

My father's magic had to be burning his arm, yet he didn't even flinch.

Dart had his daggers out and the normally happy go lucky guy looked ready to kill.

"You sleeping around already? Trying to give that demon her baby?" Dad asked.

"We're her partners from her guild," Dart said. "And I *really* want to slit your throat."

Dad's eyes widened. "I haven't done a thing to you, boy."

"No, but you've hurt her," Silas said and with a jerk of his arm, pulled the whip out of my dad's hand.

Dad gaped. No one had been able to take his whip before.

"Just leave," I said. "I don't ever want to see you again. I thought I made that clear the night I left."

"You're my child. I own you. You still owe me," Dad said.

Screw this. I didn't need to hide from him anymore. I knew Thor would hear me this time and there was no point in hiding this from him any longer.

"Thor!" I screamed up into the sky.

The next instant, Thor materialized behind my father. He grabbed my father by the throat and lifted him up off his feet. "You have many sins to pay for. First, for hurting my friend. Second, for hurting her sisters. And third, for doing it while you knew I was away."

"I didn't—"

Thor and Dad disappeared the next second, before Dad could finish whatever lie he'd been about to spout.

I slumped against the building behind us. It was finally over. He was dead. But … no my sisters…

"My family won't have food," I whispered. "That's why I never killed him. He was the only one who brought in money. I'll have to—"

"I'll handle it," Silas and Thor said at the same time.

My head jerked up, eyes wide as they found Thor. "He's dead?"

Thor nodded.

"My sisters—"

"I will handle it," Thor said and hugged me. "And, I will help you."

"What?" I asked.

He smiled, stood, and whispered something into Silas's ear. Silas's eyes widened at whatever he said, and Thor disappeared.

"What did he say?" I asked.

Silas opened his mouth and then closed it. "We can talk about it later. We need to finish our shopping."

"Silas," I snapped.

He walked to a nearby trashcan and threw my dad's whip inside it.

"You weren't hurt by his magic?" I asked, staring at the whip that had tormented me for so many years.

"A little," Silas said.

I looked up and saw the burn marks on his forearm. "You fool," I whispered and reached out towards him.

He pushed me back. "I'm fine. They'll heal before we make it back to the guild."

"Come on," Dart said, finally putting his daggers away. "One more stop."

I followed them, feeling a weight lifted from my shoulders. But, more doubt about what Thor had meant. I knew if he said he would take care of my sisters that he would, but how would he help me, too? What had he told Silas? What was he plotting, and why would he involve Silas?

I would pry it out of Silas the next time I could get him alone.

Dart led us into a supply store and I browsed around, checking out the various items that piqued my interest. There was a little of everything in here.

"Are you stalking us?" Jasper asked, his whispered words moving the hair on the back of my neck.

I looked up and smiled. "It seems our paths are destined to cross."

He smirked and leaned his shoulder against the wall. "I like the sound of that."

Dart and Silas were up at the front, far enough away that they wouldn't hear me talking to him.

"I need to be upfront about something," I said.

His smirk disappeared and he nodded. "Go on."

"I'm interested in pursuing this ... whatever it is, but I can't have kids for at least five decades. For personal reasons," I told him. "I don't know if that changes things for you and your ..."

"Friends," he supplied. "And no, that actually works well for us."

"So, you still want me to meet you for dinner? All three of you?" I asked.

He smiled. "We do everything together." Leaning close he whispered in my ear, "Including women."

Shivers raced up my spine and heat flushed my cheeks and lower body. Wow.

"Six o'clock?" I asked.

He nodded and stepped back. "Six o'clock."

I glanced over at Silas and Dart who were finishing up with their purchases. "I might be a bit late."

He smiled. "We'll wait for you."

"I won't leave my guild," I said quickly as he turned to leave.

He arched a brow. "I didn't say anything about your guild."

"I know, I'm just saying I won't. Even if this …
progresses."

He smiled. "Ah, understood. See you tonight, Nadia."

He left and I felt joy fill me. Joy and nervousness. I
hadn't dated a guy in years. Let alone three at the same
time.

"You okay?" Dart asked.

I nodded and headed towards the door. "Yep. I'm great."

8

Darkness descended and the clock moved closer to six. We had come back to the guild and I'd changed into one of my new outfits. I even brushed my hair.

Then, I snuck out the back and headed towards town.

Halfway there, Dart snuck up on my left. "Where are we going?"

I yelped and jumped sideways … into Silas.

I groaned. "You guys. What are you doing here?"

"Well, we saw you sneaking out and thought we should join the fun," Dart said.

"I'm not sneaking out or … well …"

"Where are you going?" Silas asked.

"I'm going on a date," I said, watching his face.

A stone mask covered up any expression he might have made.

"With those guys?" Dart asked.

I nodded.

"One or all of them?" Silas asked. The mask slipped, revealing irritation.

"Look, I just wanted to get out for a bit and they offered to take me for dinner. I'll be back. I promise I'm just going to dinner with them. And, I already told them I won't be leaving our guild, no matter what. Okay?"

"Of course you aren't leaving the guild," Dart said and shook his head. "You're stuck with us."

I smiled. "Or, you're stuck with me."

He shrugged. "Either way."

"So, I appreciate you coming after me, but I'll be going on my date now. Bye."

I waved to them and picked up my pace, but they kept walking behind me.

"What are you doing?" I asked with a groan, turning to face them and walked backwards.

"Going to dinner," Silas said.

I pointed at the guild. "You eat dinner there."

"I'm tired of dinner there. I want to eat out," Silas said with a smile.

"You're coming to spy on me," I gaped.

"We would never spy on you," Dart said with his mouth open and a hand to his chest.

"You are so spying on me. Fine. Whatever. I don't care. Just don't interfere, okay?" I looked pointedly at Silas.

"Why would I interfere with your date?" he asked.

"Because you keep glaring daggers at them every time they come talk to me," I said.

"Do not," he countered.

"You totally do," Dart said. Silas shot him a look, but Dart just shrugged. "You do."

Resigned, I turned back around and hurried to the cafe, making it there right at six.

The three guys were at a table with one chair open.

I sat down and they smiled at me, but their smiles didn't last long when they saw Silas and Dart walk in and take a seat at a table on the other side of the room.

"They're stalking me," I said. "They're worried you're trying to convince me to go with you to your guild, since it was my first choice originally."

"Our guild would love to have you," Grayson said.

I shook my head. "Too late."

"You look lovely," Jasper said. "I like the shirt."

"Thanks," I said, not sure how to reply.

"So, tell us about your mission," Parker said.

I told them about the mission, but left out my dad showing up or Silas getting mad at me for charging in to save the old man. Then, I asked them to tell me about theirs.

"It was a level six," Grayson said. "We had a little trouble fighting the trolls, but a few good cuts to their tendons made it easier to take them down."

"How many trolls did you kill?" I asked.

Grayson looked at Parker and Jasper.

Parker counted on his fingers. "Six."

My mouth dropped. "You three defeated six trolls?"

"Yeah," Grayson said. "I'm sure you could have defeated more."

I shook my head. "No way. I doubt I could defeat one."

"Your magic rating says otherwise," Jasper countered.

I shook my head again. "That doesn't translate over to being able to defeat enemies. I can't use all my power at once."

"Why not?"

"It gets … unstable," I said since I didn't want to admit I couldn't control myself when I used all of my power.

"More like glorious," Loki said as he pulled a chair up and sat beside me.

I let my head fell forward and groaned. "No."

"Hello, beautiful. It's been such a long time since I last saw you," Loki purred.

"You know the Trickster?" Grayson asked.

"Grayson, what have I said about using my nickname?" Loki chastised him.

"Wait. You guys know him?" I asked, raising my head.

"Oh, you haven't told her yet. This is exciting. Go on, tell her," Loki said, his smile wide and eyes sparkling while he set his chin on his clasped hands atop the table and looked between us expectantly. He looked like a kid in an ice cream store waiting for his cone to be handed to him.

"He's … our grandfather," Jasper said.

Every muscle in me tensed. Please don't let them be Hel's.

"Who is your mother?" I asked.

"Hel," all three said.

I covered my face with my hands and Loki laughed loudly, clapping his hands together like it was the best joke he had ever heard.

"Wait, you said you were friends," I accused Jasper.

"Half-brothers," he said. "It's easier to say friends."

"Son of a—"

Loki put his hand over my mouth. "Language, Nadia."

I rolled my eyes.

He leaned over and whispered, "If you had called for

me, I would have helped with your father. We may bicker, but I despise men like that."

I stared with wide eyes. Loki would have helped me?

"Boys, do you remember the girl your mom talked about? The one who tricked Thor into a contract to be her friend?" Loki asked.

There was the jerk I knew so well. "I didn't trick him. He didn't read the contract."

The three guys looked at me. Grayson looked impressed. Jasper looked shocked. Parker looked unconvinced.

"That was you?" Parker asked.

Thor appeared behind Loki. "What did I tell you about harassing Nadia?"

"She's harassing my grandsons," Loki said and stood.

"I'm not harassing them. They invited me," I said defensively.

Thor narrowed his eyes at me. "You won't help me make demigods, but you'll date them?"

"I already told them I don't want kids," I said, heat burning my cheeks.

"You know Hel won't approve of this," Thor said.

"Mom doesn't get a say in who we date," Parker countered.

"You better not let your mom kill her," Thor growled.

Grayson turned serious for the first time since I had met them. "We won't let Mom hurt her."

Loki leaned over and whispered, "Run while you can."

I narrowed my eyes at him. "I don't run from challenges."

He scowled and said, "You should learn to."

Before I could respond, he and Thor disappeared.

"Mom knows not to interfere in our love lives," Jasper said. "So, don't worry about it."

"Your mom really hates me," I said. "For more than the stupid contract."

Grayson shrugged and smiled again. "We make our own decisions about people. Most think our grandfather is a bad god. We know different."

Why did it feel like everything was trying to push me away from these guys?

And why did that make them even more enticing and make me even more determined to see where this went?

"You're seriously screwed up," Norma muttered.

"Says the demon holding my magic hostage because she can't accomplish the things I can," I replied in my head.

She growled.

"So," I said. "How old are you three?"

"Twenty-three," Grayson said.

"Twenty-two," Parker said.

"Twenty-four," Jasper said.

"You joined a guild late, too," I commented.

Jasper scowled. "Took us a while to convince Mom."

I could see Hel being very protective of her kids.

That did not make me any less nervous.

"Let's order food," Parker said and raised his hand so the waitress would come over to us.

We made small talk throughout dinner and yet things felt strained.

Maybe this wouldn't work after all. Maybe this wasn't meant to be, and even though I kept bumping into them and felt so comfortable around them, it was just purely coincidence.

We walked out of the cafe and to the river.

Silas and Dart watched from the cafe balcony.

"I'm sorry tonight's been something of a disaster," I said, sighing. Maybe I should just stay single.

"Let's make it better then," Jasper said and held out his hand.

Silas stood and started towards us.

I set my hand in Jasper's and the world tilted around me.

Spinning stars circled overhead, I almost threw up, but I managed to hold it in.

Jasper pulled me against his chest and the feeling lessened.

I'd traveled on the rainbow bridge before, but Thor had always held me. Now I knew why.

It stopped and I opened my eyes to find a world unlike mine. The sky was purple and the grass was a teal-ish blue. Buildings three times as high as ours made up a city below.

Tilting my head back, I met Jasper's gaze.

He smiled and brushed my hair behind my ear. "Welcome to Jotunheim."

The home of the Jotun, the giants.

That explained the tall buildings.

Parker and Grayson appeared beside us.

"It's beautiful," I whispered.

Parker took my hand and led me down the hill we stood on, towards the city.

Thor had told me about Jotunheim before, but it was so much more beautiful than he had described.

Looking up, I took in the stars and planets. It was such a different view than from Midgard.

I stumbled a step and Parker wrapped his arm around my waist and pulled me against his side. He was so warm and smelled like cherries. All of them smelled like cherries. Did they eat a lot of cherries or was it just their scent?

"Sorry, I shouldn't stargaze and walk," I said, smiling up at him.

His eyes were glued to mine for a few heartbeats and then he asked, "Would you like to stand a moment and look at them?"

"Personally, I think my view is much more beautiful," Grayson said from beside me.

I turned my head to look at him, his eyes focused on me.

Stepping back from the trio, I let myself breathe. I continued smiling and turned towards the town. "You three are far too smooth. How many hapless virgins have you deflowered?"

"We aren't concerned with the past. Just our current goal," Grayson said.

"What goal is that?" I asked without facing them.

They fell into step beside me, Grayson on my left, Parker on my right, and Jasper on Parker's right.

"If we revealed that, it would impede our goal," Parker said.

"If you're hoping to deflower me, you're in for a sad discovery," I said.

"Oh, this goal far exceeds deflowering," Jasper said.

I tensed, my thoughts running wild with things they could be planning, including my murder.

We were on a different planet. I could summon Thor, but it would take him time to get here and they might kill me in that time.

"The thoughts in your head do not appear pleasant," Grayson said.

I knew I was more powerful than them individually, but if they teamed up, I wasn't so sure I could win.

"She finds trusting difficult and thinks the worst of people," Norma said from my mouth.

"Fucking, Norma. Don't do that," I snapped and my body shuddered.

"Was that the demon?" Jasper asked.

I sighed and nodded. "Don't worry, she can't control my body, just my mouth when my defenses are down."

A giant and giantess lay on the grass ahead, their hands interlaced.

At our approach, they sat up.

The giantess smiled at the boys. "What are you three doing here?"

"We brought our friend to meet Angrboda," Jasper said.

The giantess looked at me. "You're touched by Aesir magic. Who guards you?"

"Thunderer," Grayson said before I could say his name.

The giant's eyes narrowed. "She also smells of darkness."

"*I do not smell,*" Norma huffed.

"Keep her away from Barno. He's in a mood," the giantess said.

After we were far enough away that the couple wouldn't hear, I turned to Jasper. "You didn't say anything about meeting anyone."

He smiled. "No, I didn't."

"Who is Angrboda?" I asked. The name sounded familiar, but I couldn't place it.

He draped his arm around me and said, "Don't worry, she'll love you."

I narrowed my eyes at him and he just smiled wider.

9

The town was very similar to ours, just on a larger scale.

I'd never felt so small.

The guys walked through the town like they owned it.

Giants and giantesses watched us, but there was no hatred, just curiosity and familiarity.

They stopped at a house with flowers of blues and purples lining the front. It was cute and reminded me of a cottage.

Grayson threw open the door and yelled, "Angrboda, we're home."

"My boys!" a giantess yelled and walked out of the kitchen. She had a pretty purple dress on and an apron covered in flour over that. She even had flour in her hair. Her smile disappeared when she saw me. "Who's this?"

"This is Nadia," Jasper pushed me forward, ahead of them to stand on my own before her.

"Hello," I said, and bowed as low as I could. "Your home is very lovely."

She squatted down to look at me. "That's an old spell

holding your magic. I wonder how such a young demon got her hands on it."

Young? And how could she even see it?

Norma was surprisingly quiet.

"How long have you been dating them?" she asked.

"Tonight's our first date, actually," I said, my shock making me answer her instead of asking all the questions I wanted to.

Her eyes widened and she stood. "Grayson, come help me in the kitchen. Jasper, you and Parker take her to the living room."

Parker took my hand and tugged gently. "Come on." He led me to a living room and I imagined this must be what bugs felt like in our homes.

I looked at the couch and wondered how I was going to get up on it. If I ran and jumped … maybe.

Parker picked me up in his arms and jumped onto the couch.

Wide-eyed, I silently stared at him.

He set me down and sat beside me, setting his arm around my shoulders. "We lived here most of our lives. We got really good at jumping."

"I see that," I said.

Jasper sat next to me and scowled at Parker's arm. After a second of thought, he reached down and linked our hands together. The scowl was replaced with a smile and he relaxed against the couch.

They were rather physically affectionate, especially on a first date, but since they hadn't crossed any lines, I let it stand.

"Is she a relative?" I asked.

Both nodded, but offered nothing else.

Grayson and Angrboda came back into the room with a tray of huge cookies.

Grayson jumped up and settled beside Jasper.

She broke a cookie into fourths, the pieces still twice as large as any cookie I had ever eaten, and handed us each a piece. She sat in a reclining chair, folded her hands in her lap, and asked, "What are your intentions with my grandsons?"

My mouth almost dropped open, but I clamped it shut and swallowed hard.

She was Hel's mom.

"I don't really know," I said, once the shock wore off. "We only met a few times before. They sort of attached themselves to me."

She looked at their arm and hand on me. "I see that. Yet, you aren't pushing them away."

"They accepted that I don't want to have kids and that I have a demon problem easily. That's not something most guys would do."

She smiled. "They don't want kids. And they've dealt with their fair share of demons."

"How can you see the demon and her container?" I asked, leaning forward a bit.

She shrugged. "How can Thunderer summon lightning? We just can."

"Mom doesn't like her," Jasper said.

She rolled her eyes. "She doesn't like anyone."

"Can you help her?" Grayson asked.

"I don't—" I began, but stopped when Jasper squeezed my hand.

"Perhaps, but have you asked her if she wants to be helped?"

Three sets of eyes turned to me.

"Why wouldn't you want help?" Parker asked.

"It's not so much that I don't want help as it is, I don't want to trouble anyone else for my screw up. I'll fix this one way or another."

"How many years left?" Angrboda asked.

"Thirty six."

"It isn't weakness to accept help." She smiled warmly at me and I wondered if this was what it might be like to have a caring mother-figure in your life.

No responses came to mind, so I looked down at my lap instead, eating the cookie silently as they spoke with her.

How could I admit that I also didn't want help removing Norma because I wanted to help her? To admit we had some similar goals?

"We should head back," Grayson said. "Your partners are probably worried."

Jasper scooped me up and jumped down to the floor.

They moved and changed topics almost as quickly as Dart.

I bowed to Angrboda. "Thank you for your hospitality."

"I hope to see you again soon," she said. "In the meantime, you should learn to control your magic and learn to actually let people in. Your walls are thick. If you opened them, you'd be surprised what love can accomplish ... including breaking things open."

Grayson led us out of the house and back through the town, while I mulled over what she had said.

What had she meant about love breaking things open?

Did she mean Norma's container? No. Emotions couldn't break things, except hearts.

We were almost out of the town when a giant stepped in our way. He snarled and asked, "Why is a Midgardian here?"

"We're leaving," Grayson said.

The giant reached for me.

The three brothers suddenly grew in size, becoming the same size as the giant.

My mouth dropped and I stared in total shock.

Parker grabbed me, picking my entire body up in one hand, and ran around the giant.

Jasper and Grayson fought the giant back and once Parker and I were far enough away, they followed.

The giant didn't follow, just glared and wiped blood from his chin.

We reached the hill we had arrived on and Parker set me down. Then, all three shrank back to their normal sizes.

"Whoa," I said, impressed.

10

We arrived just outside The Golden Alicorn territory.

Grayson smiled down at me. "Well, tonight was fun."

I chuckled. "It was definitely interesting and informative."

He kissed my lips, just a quick peck before releasing me.

Jasper stepped up and brushed his thumb over my lower lip. "We have a mission in a couple of days and we might not be back for a week or two."

"Okay," I said breathlessly, lost in his eyes.

He kissed me, released me, and Parker immediately pulled me into a hug. "We will come find you when we're back."

"Have fun on your mission," I said and tilted my head so I could look up at him. He kissed me hard, pulling me tight against his body.

When he released me, my entire body tingled and I felt cold without his touch.

"Stay safe," he whispered and stepped back one step and then another.

We waved to each other as we turned in opposite directions, my mind reeling from the insane number of events that had happened so quickly. And why did I feel cold now that I was away from them? Why was I reacting to strangely to these … strangers?

As soon as I stepped onto Golden Alicorn grounds, the front door of the main house opened and Silas stepped out.

I waved and walked to him.

"Where have you been?" he asked, looking me over.

"Another planet," I said, and squeezed by him.

"You let those guys, you barely know, take you to another planet?" He followed me up the stairs to my room.

I turned and arched a brow. "So?"

"They could have done any number of things, including abandon you there. You don't know if you can trust them."

"Silas, they're demigods. If they did anything, Thor would have their heads."

"You can't expect Thor to drop everything and come save you," he snapped, his hands clenched into fists at his sides.

Fury consumed me, as did pain. The doors lining the hallway opened and everyone looked out.

"I'm well aware that Thor isn't always able to protect me," I snapped back.

Silas dropped his eyes.

"I went through years of pain at the hands of my father to drill that fact into my head. Thanks for the reminder after a fun night, though." I closed my door on him and collapsed into bed.

Why was he being such a jerk? I didn't do anything wrong.

Plus, I was a freaking adult. I didn't need his permission to go out and I didn't need him treating me like a child.

"*He likes you,*" Norma said. "*He's jealous.*"

"Well, he can get over it," I muttered. "I only have one life and I intend to live it to the fullest."

After a fitful night of sleep, I found Dart and dragged him to choose a mission.

Silas had been with him, so he followed as well.

Overnight, I'd lost my anger towards Silas. He had been worried and said things without thinking. I did that often enough and knew I wouldn't want someone holding it against me.

Standing before the boards, I glanced at Silas. "Any catch your eye?"

His eyes widened and he pointed to one.

I read it and before Dart could even respond, I grabbed it. "Perfect. Meet out front in thirty."

Since I wasn't sure how long we'd be gone, I packed enough for a week.

Silas and Dart waited out front, packs on, whispering to each other.

I smiled wide. "Ready?"

"Yes," Dart said, returning my smile. "Adventuring!" He pumped his fist in the air.

Silas chuckled and we walked towards town.

"Why the rush to do another mission?" Dart asked.

I shrugged. "What else are we going to do? I'd rather work and earn money than sit around."

"So, what is our mission? You took the card before I could read it." Dart walked in front of Silas and me, backwards so he could see us.

"Monster hunting," I said with a wide smile.

His eyes lit up. "Really?"

I nodded. "A huge monster keeps coming out of the forest and terrorizing the nearby town."

"We'll need to talk to the townspeople to find out if there's a pattern and if there is a possible reason for the repeated attacks," Silas said.

"*You chose this job because you know I love monster fighting, didn't you?*" Norma asked.

"*Maybe,*" I said telepathically.

"*Careful, I'm starting to like you.*"

I chuckled. "That would be most unfortunate."

"She's talking to the demoness again, isn't she?" Dart asked Silas.

Both watched me with furrowed brows.

I smiled. "Norma likes killing monsters."

"I thought you said she can't take over your body?" Silas asked.

"She can't, but she can enjoy me killing it and live vicariously through me," I explained.

"Why doesn't she just come here and fight herself?" Dart asked.

Because she can't take her revenge and kill the demons after her without me.

"It's complicated," I answered and shrugged, not wanting to get into it with him.

We continued on our way to take a portal and I felt lighter for some reason. I shouldn't have felt so light when I had a million things weighing on my mind, but I did.

Why were Thor and Loki suddenly getting involved in my life again? Was it because of bumping into the trio?

What was their motive in dating me? Would they hurt me to please their mother?

I barely knew them and yet felt like I could trust them, which was definitely not how I normally felt about people. I felt like I should avoid them and yet wanted to run to them at the same time. It was frustrating.

Shoving all that aside, I thought about the payout from this job. It would be enough to buy a new sword and have my daggers sharpened. There would even be a bit left over that I could save.

One of the other reasons I'd wanted to join a guild was because they offered free housing and food. After having gone so long without decent food, and sometimes without food at all, I was incredibly grateful to the chefs at the Golden Alicorn.

That was something else I could buy with my earnings … treats! I'd kill for a piece of cake.

I chuckled as I realized that technically I was killing for a piece of cake now. Killing a monster anyways.

"What are you chuckling about?" Dart asked.

"It's stupid," I said and shook my head.

He bumped his arm into mine. "I love stupid."

"I was thinking how I'd kill for a piece of cake, since I never get to eat sweets because they're expensive. Then I realized I am killing for cake by killing the monster and using the money to buy cake later."

Dart's brows furrowed a moment before he threw his head back and boomed with laughter. "You're right! I never thought about it that way before!"

Silas smirked, but said nothing as we moved into the line to wait for our turn to use the portal.

We made it through the portal without incident, which only made me smile wider.

My dad was finally dead. He wouldn't hurt me or my sisters ever again.

At some point, I'd need to go visit them, but that could wait until I had some savings and could bring them treats.

The town before us was pretty similar to the one we'd been at for our first mission, but the forest behind this town oozed darkness.

"*That's not a normal monster in there,*" Norma whispered.

"Is the forest cursed?" I wondered aloud.

"Could be," Dart whispered. "It definitely doesn't feel right."

Silas nodded. "Either the forest, town, or monster is cursed."

"I'm not good with removing curses," I admitted. "Killing is my preferred method."

"Let's talk to the townspeople and see if we can learn more from them," Silas said. "We can figure out our strategy once we have more information."

Dart and I nodded our agreement and the three of us headed into the town.

As soon as we entered the town, all of our eyebrows rose into our hairlines.

The townspeople were smiling, looked well-fed, had beautiful outfits on, and looked as if they hadn't a care in the world.

Silas talked with some of the people while Dart and I walked around, trying to eavesdrop on conversations or spot something out of the ordinary.

"Are you as creeped out as me?" I asked Dart as softly as possible.

He nodded, while his eyes focused on two men talking near the water fountain. The men were smiling, but the corners of their eyes were pinched.

"Can you hear what they're saying?" I asked while watching two women walk by. The two women walked behind Silas and started whispering and giggling.

Yes, Silas is handsome. Keep moving.

"They're talking about a curfew," Dart whispered. "They seem worried, but they're smiling like they aren't."

Silas whistled once before heading out of the town.

I pushed off the wall and followed after him with Dart right behind me.

Once we were far enough away from the town, we huddled together.

"There's definitely something fishy going on here," Silas said, talking in a hushed tone even though we were far enough away that the townspeople couldn't hear us even if we shouted. "No one knew what I was talking about when I mentioned the monster or the job."

"There were two men discussing a curfew, but still acted happy and carefree," Dart added.

"The corners of their eyes were pinched," I said.

We stared at each other, trying to understand what could possibly be going on.

"Um, excuse me," a soft female voice called from behind a tree on Silas's left.

We all looked at her, and tensed.

Had she heard us? Was she going to tell the townspeople?

"Are you from a guild?" she asked, looking around nervously. She looked like she was no older than thirteen, thin, and had a faded bruise on her chin and one on her throat. Her clothing was clean and had no tears or stains that I could see, though.

"Yes, we're from Golden Alicorn," Silas answered in a surprisingly tender voice.

She wiggled her finger at us and stepped behind the tree.

"Should one of us stay here in case it's a trap?" Dart asked.

Silas nodded. "Dart, stay here. Nadia, come with me."

I followed at his side, my senses on high alert.

This area of trees didn't feel corrupted like the rest. So, it was probably safe to go in.

Silas took the first step and with no noticeable issues, I followed as well.

Once we were hidden from the town by the trees, the girl looked up at us sheepishly.

"How can we help you?" Silas asked her.

"I'm the one who submitted the request," she said in a hushed whisper.

"What's going on with them?" I asked her. "They said they didn't know anything about a monster."

"That's because it put a spell on them. During the day, they don't remember what happens. At night, the monster comes out and attacks," she explained.

"The town doesn't look like it's in repairs. What does it do?" I asked.

Her hands fisted in her dress. "If anyone is outside, it takes them and eats them. If no one is outside, it lures someone out. It's been taking the oldest person."

Now that she said that, I realized there hadn't been any elderly people in the town. The oldest person had looked to be in their late forties.

"When did this start?" Silas asked.

"About a month ago," she said, her eyes darting around nervously. "Something happened, but the elders refused to discuss it or let anyone else discuss whatever it was. Then, the monster started coming and they became even more tight-lipped. I heard someone say they think the monster's baby was killed by one of the people in our town, but I wouldn't think that it would continue attacking so many times. It doesn't seem like it is going to stop the attacks anytime soon, either."

There was something about her story that seemed off to me, but I couldn't put my finger on what it was exactly. "At night, do the others remember about the monster?" I asked.

She nodded. "As soon as the sun starts to set, they gather in their homes and discuss ways to try to stop it. Some are discussing moving completely, but they'd have to move during the night, since as soon as the sun rises, they forget all about the monster again."

"How come you aren't affected by the spell?" Silas asked.

"None of the kids are," she answered. "We don't know why, but only the adults forget during the day. Unfortunately, none of us are very powerful, so we have no hopes of fighting back. That's why I sent out the call for aid."

"What's the monster look like? What powers does it have?" I asked. The sooner we killed this thing, the sooner the townspeople would be safe and we could go back home.

Dart whistled and Silas told me to go to him while he talked with the girl more about the creature.

"What's up?" I asked Dart, who was still facing the town.

"Some of the teenagers met up in the middle of town, frowning and talking animatedly," he said. "They're the only ones I've seen show an emotion other than happiness."

I nodded and then explained what the girl had told us.

His brows furrowed as he continued to watch the people move about. "I've heard of something similar happening."

"What was the cause?" I asked.

His foot tapped on the ground a few times while he thought. "I'm trying to remember. I think it had to do with a bargain." He started heading towards the hill that overlooked the town, giving us space from the people so we could talk openly without worry they would overhear us.

"A bargain with the monster?" I asked.

He shook his head. "No, with someone else who controlled the monster."

"Controlled the monster? You think someone could be controlling this monster?" I knew there were some people who made bargains with demons and then could use the monster to attack people, but normally those were short lived contracts due to the demon killing the person soon after. There were some who had magic that would let them mind control creatures for a short period of time, but to have a monster attack every night for a month was outside the magic power I'd seen so far.

"It's possible," he whispered.

"That's terrifying," I whispered back.

Silas came over to where we were, sat on the ground, and let out a huge sigh. "This is not going to be easy. We might have to call in backup."

Thinking about asking for help made my hackles rise. I didn't want anyone to die, but … "We should try killing it tonight and if we need help, call for backup first thing tomorrow," I suggested.

Dart smirked, but said nothing.

Silas scowled and after a moment said, "It's probably not a good idea to pull someone this late in the day anyway. I'd prefer to have plenty of planning time with them instead of calling them straight into a fight."

Dart and I nodded our agreement.

"So, how are we going to fight this thing?" I asked Silas.

"Let me think about it. I'm still mulling over what she said," he muttered, lay on his back, and closed his eyes.

I looked at Dart, who shrugged.

I shrugged back and lay down on the grass with my eyes closed to nap. No point in using energy unnecessarily.

"*I have a feeling tonight is going to be a lot of fun,*" Norma whispered.

I rolled my eyes without response.

Demons craved chaos and violence. So, it was no surprise that she wanted to see what this monster could do. I just hoped we were able to defeat it relatively easily.

"*You don't want them calling in reinforcements because you don't want to split up that payment any more than it already is,*" Norma commented.

She wasn't wrong, but I wouldn't admit it aloud.

"This bothers me," Silas said. "I want to know what the adults did to make the monster attack."

"Maybe the monster will tell us while we're fighting it," I suggested with a smirk.

Silas snorted.

"So, what planet did you go to?" Dart asked.

"Huh?" I asked, opening one eye to look at him.

He'd sat down beside me, but his gaze was still focused on the town. "On your date. You said they took you to another planet. Which one?"

"Jotunheimr," I answered because I didn't have anything to hide from them.

"Where the giants live?" he asked.

"Yep."

"Did the giants care you were there?" he asked.

"Only one of them was upset and the guys protected me from him," I said. "Most of the others knew the guys because they visit there often."

While I didn't have anything to hide regarding myself, I wasn't going to give out personal information about the guys.

"It was really pretty," I added. "I've seen some of the other planets with Thor and Loki, but I've never really gotten to spend much time there. I want to have a vacation at some of them to have time to really explore it."

"You realize that ninety-eight percent of the jobs we do are on Midgard, right?" Silas asked.

I nodded. "I know. Doesn't change me wanting to go to other places for vacations."

"It would be nice to explore other planets," Dart agreed. He turned, met my eyes, and smiled wide. "Maybe we can have a team vacation! That way the three of us are together and can have each other's backs if something goes wrong."

"Sounds awesome," I said. "Though, I think someone might be a spoilsport and yell at us trying to have fun."

"I know you're talking about me and I'm offended. I'm not a stick in the mud," Silas grumbled.

I glanced over at him and smirked. "Have you ever broken the law before?"

He scowled. "No. Why would I? You can still have fun while obeying laws."

I looked up at Dart and as soon as our eyes connected, we burst into laughter.

"I figured she was going to be trouble, but I did not anticipate you being trouble as well," Silas said to Dart.

Dart rolled his eyes. "I like having fun as much as the next person. Plus, some places have really stupid laws that are just there to protect the wealthy from having to deal with those of us without money."

"Exactly," I agreed and nodded vigorously.

"Maybe trios was a bad idea," Silas grumbled.

"You'd be worried sick if Nadia and I were out by ourselves. It would take maybe an hour of you pacing before you ran after us," Dart said smugly.

Silas made noises, but didn't say anything.

We all knew Dart was right.

"I don't need a babysitter," I muttered and closed my eyes so I didn't have to see their faces.

12

"How did you get mixed up with the gods anyway?" Dart asked.

"When I was a kid, I stayed away from home during the day, hiding in the fields and trying to find some sunshine. I was in a really isolated field one day when a horde of dark elves ran through a portal right beside me. Thor and Loki were right on their heels, having chased them across two other planets. The elves grabbed me, attempting to use me to force Thor and Loki to back down."

"What happened?" Silas asked, sitting upright and staring intently at me.

"Loki laughed at them – doubled over clutching his stomach laughed. The dark elf holding me relaxed his hold and I used my magic to shock him to fully release me. As soon as I was released, I ran straight towards Thor and Loki. Loki threw a few daggers, used his magic to teleport, and grabbed me. Then, Thor used Mjolnir and his powers to break the ground and send waves of lightning into the elves, staggering them."

"Wait, you're saying Loki *saved* you?" Dart asked, brows furrowed.

I nodded. "As soon as Thor finished off the dark elves, Loki tossed me to him and disappeared. Thor took me to Asgard when I refused to tell him where my parents were. I wrote the contract and he signed it. At the time we had no idea what the implications would be years later, but here we are."

"So, Loki doesn't hate you," Silas said.

I shrugged. "He's hard to read, but he does have a heart and has done a lot for me over the years. Hel hates me, but that's a long story I don't want to get into."

"What are your plans and goals?" Silas asked. "You've joined a guild. Now what?"

"I do jobs, save money, try to increase my power and skill, and survive," I answered honestly. Sure, there was more to it than that, but he didn't need to know my plans with Norma. "Alright, I've told you a lot about myself. Time for you to tell us a story," I ordered Dart.

He shrugged. "I'm not very interesting. My parents weren't rich, but we never went without. I joined a guild late because I was more focused on my studies than joining. I realized that I was lonely and knew if I joined a guild that I wouldn't be alone anymore." He smiled wide. "And I was totally right. As soon as I saw you in line at the drafts, I knew it was destiny."

I felt my checks heat and looked over at Silas. "Your turn."

Silas scowled, his eyes darkening as he stared at the town. "I don't talk about my past because it's just that ... the past. It doesn't matter now."

"But it made you who you are," I whispered. "And knowing where you came from can help us better understand who you are today."

His scowl softened and he looked over at me. "That was pretty deep."

I lightly punched his shoulder. "I do have deep thoughts, you know?"

"So, you just want a story about my past?" he asked.

Dart and I nodded.

Silas stared off into space. Just when I thought he wouldn't tell us something, he started to speak. "When I was a child, my stepfather would abuse my mother. I spent all of my spare time learning spells and increasing my power. When I was thirteen, he tried to hit her in front of me and I blacked out. When I came to, our house was destroyed, my stepfather was dead, and my mother and sisters were cowering at my feet. They said power just exploded out of me and obliterated everything. My stepfather had been powerful, but apparently not as powerful as I was. I should probably feel bad about it, but I don't. He was an abusive jerk and deserved his fate. The only thing I do regret is that my sisters and mother never met my eyes after that, fearing I would be like him, even though I had never in my life raised my hand against them. They still won't meet my eyes whenever I do see them."

He saved his sisters and mother and they were scared of him? I supposed I could see them being wary of a male after suffering at their father's hands. I wasn't sure what to say to him. What could I say to lighten the mood?

"Well, I think you're awesome and will make all kinds of eye contact with you," Dart said with a wide smile.

Silas smirked and I let out a breath quietly.

Thank you, Dart.

"You're so awkward," Norma muttered.

"Shut it," I hissed in my head.

"Your turn," Silas said to Dart.

Dart tapped his finger against his lips a few times, eyes unfocused. "What to tell. What story. Hm."

Silas and I remained quiet, watching the town and the forest beyond.

"When I was six years old, I was swimming with some friends in a river near my house, our horses tied up at the top of the hill. There was a landslide upriver that none of us knew about and it sent a huge wave of water and debris downriver, right to where we were. I was the only one in the water at the time, thankfully, and got swept downriver at incredible speeds. I tried to swim to safety, but the fallen trees started slamming into me and I lost consciousness a few times. I thought I was a goner; certain I was going to die. My friends had grabbed the horses and tried to race ahead, but the water was just too fast."

"What happened?" I asked. I mean, obviously he survived, but how?

"A goddess appeared before me, pulled me from the water, drew the water from my lungs, and blew a warm breath that instantly dried me," he explained, a soft smile on his lips.

"Which goddess?" I asked curiously.

"Epona," he answered. "She said that the horses had called out to her because they were trying so hard to save me, but just weren't fast enough. She explained that my horse loved me so much that she had almost jumped into the river after me, but my friends had stopped her, and that anyone who earned an equine love like that deserved to be saved."

"I've never heard of a goddess named Epona," I admitted with a frown.

He smirked. "She's not part of Thor's pantheon."

My eyes widened, my mouth dropped open, and I just stared at him. Other gods? More pantheons?

"You didn't know?" Silas asked.

"How many others are there?" I asked, my voice barely a whisper.

"At least a dozen," Loki said from behind us.

I spun around, dagger in my hand, and glared at him.

He smiled. "Hello, Nadia."

"What are you doing here?" I asked and tightened my hold on my dagger. I was not about to let my guard down.

He stuck his bottom lip out in a pout. "Is that anyway to talk to your future grandfather-in-law?"

My eyes narrowed as I glared at him. "That's totally not decided yet. One date, Loki. I've only been on one date with them."

He waved his hand dismissively. "Whatever. I know them and I know you and you were practically made for each other. I always knew you were too much and would need more than one mate. I'm curious how many you'll gather, though. I doubt it will just be those three."

My cheeks warmed and my teeth ground together, but words wouldn't come out.

"Why are you here?" Dart asked after a glance at me.

Loki arched a brow. "You do realize I'm a god, right?"

"Loki," I growled.

He dropped a purple crystal and it hovered in front of me. "I promised the boys that I'd assist you and keep you from getting killed. They don't know you well, and yet they know you have a propensity for getting yourself into trouble."

I stared at the crystal curiously, but didn't touch it. "What is it?"

He smiled. "You'll see. Just make sure you're holding on to it when the sun sets, which is in about ten minutes, and do not let go under any circumstances. You have to keep hold of it and give it to my grandsons the next time you see them."

"What does it do?" I asked.

He winked and disappeared.

"You think it's safe to use that?" Silas asked as he bent to inspect the crystal, which had fallen onto the grass after Loki disappeared.

"He loves his family, so I don't doubt that he'd do something to keep me safe if his grandsons asked," I grumbled. "I'm irritated they asked him, but I'll handle that when I see them again."

"You do seem to have a habit of getting in trouble," Silas muttered beneath his breath, almost too quiet for me to hear.

"Yeah, if you were on a mission with those guys, I'd ask them to keep an eye on you, too," Dart said and gave me a huge smile.

I squatted down, grabbed the crystal, and tensed, waiting for it to shock me or something. When nothing happened, I put it in my pocket. Even though he wouldn't get me killed, I had no doubt that there was some trick involved with this crystal. I really hoped I was able to keep all my limbs at least.

"He's right, the sun is setting and should be down soon. Let's get ready for whatever is about to come our way," Silas said.

Dart and I nodded our agreement and double checked our gear. I took the crystal out of my pocket and held it firmly in my hand. He said I needed to hold it, and I was pretty sure he didn't mean just keep it on my person.

"Things could turn sideways real fast with Loki being involved," I commented. "Be on your guard at all times."

"I'm always on guard," Silas commented.

Dart and I looked at each other, grins forming at the same time.

Oh, Silas had just made a huge mistake because now we were fully prepared to begin pranking Silas and trying to scare him.

"What are those grins for?" he asked with a scowl.

"Nothing," Dart and I replied simultaneously, our smiles widening.

Silas sighed and shook his head, but said nothing else.

"So, what do you think this monster looks like?" I asked.

"A goat," Dart said immediately.

Silas and I stared at him expectantly.

"Goats are creepy," Dart muttered and started throwing a dagger up into the air and catching it by the handle in his hand.

"Well, someday when you're comfortable, please tell us the story of how a goat traumatized you," I said with a smirk.

He gave me a glare and turned back to face the town.

The sun dropped behind the trees and we all held our breaths.

The crystal in my hand vibrated a second and the three of us waited for it to do more, but it went silent.

"I have a bad feeling about this," Silas whispered.

"Norma," I whispered.

"*Right,*" she said and released my powers.

My hair glowed; the rainbow colors cast other rainbows on the ground around us.

Dart and Silas stared at me with expressions I couldn't read.

"Ready?" I asked them.

They both blinked twice before nodding and turned away from me.

"*They like you,*" Norma said, making the L sound long.

"*I'm not ugly and have boobs, of course they think I'm attractive,*" I said mentally to her. "*That doesn't mean they like me or want anything other than in my pants.*"

"*You're so naïve,*" she said with a sigh.

"*Says the demon who made a deal with a child,*" I muttered.

"*You better make this hunt fun,*" she growled. "*Or I'm going to seal your powers up for a month.*"

My mouth dropped at her threat because I could sense her sincerity.

"What?" Dart asked.

"The demon is being a jerk," I muttered.

"Your powers seem to be active," Silas commented.

I nodded. "Yeah, they are, but … never mind." I was not going to rehash that conversation for them. Not on my life.

Darkness covered the valley, the birds flew out of the

forest over our heads, and a roar shook the ground beneath us.

"Oh, snap," I whispered.

From the center of the forest, a giant goat's head rose. It opened its mouth and revealed pointed teeth as it roared again.

"Called it," Dart said through clenched teeth.

The crystal in my hand vibrated again, glowed brighter than the moon, and the creature's head whipped around to hone in on it.

"That asshole," I whispered and started running parallel to the town, hoping to draw it away so it wouldn't attack them at all. I was going to punch Loki in his handsome face the next time I saw him.

"I thought he said he was trying to protect you!" Dart yelled beside me as he kept pace.

"Having this crystal will likely keep me from dying, but that doesn't mean I won't have one crazy ass fight on my hands anyway," I told him. "He likes making me work for things and I was honestly surprised he hadn't asked me to do something crazy to prove my interest in them. They must really mean a lot to Loki for him not to mess with me that much."

The goat-monster flattened trees as it raced after me and every time it roared, I almost fell.

"Stop roaring!" I yelled at it in frustration.

"Why is it after you?" Silas asked. "I thought it was after the town?"

I held the crystal up into the air and the creature roared again. "Loki," I hissed.

"Did he steal it from the town? Were they holding it?

How did he get it? What in the mana pots is going on?" Silas was yelling at the end and I almost smiled just at his reaction.

"Split up," I ordered them.

"No," Dart and Silas snapped simultaneously.

I rolled my eyes. "If you guys hide, you can sneak attack it."

Silas grumbled, but then he and Dart peeled away from me and I was running alone.

"*You're insane,*" Norma said gleefully.

"Well, it wouldn't be entertaining if I let Silas kill the creature before you got your fill," I replied, smiling wide.

"*It is moments like this that I'm glad I suckered you into this contract, but also sad because I like you so much,*" she admitted.

I chuckled. "Careful, Norma, you're starting to sound like you might like me."

The creature finally made it out of the trees and ran at me.

"*I'm going to let you have more access than normal, but just this once,*" she told me.

I snickered. "You just want me to slice it up really well."

She didn't respond, which I took for confirmation.

When I felt we were finally far enough from the town to fight the creature without endangering them, I stopped, spun around, and hit the creature's chest with a blast of fire.

The fire scorched its fur and the goat creature roared and stomped its front legs.

"Well, I think that pissed it off more than anything," I said with a chuckle.

Dart and Silas ran out from each side and started

attacking the creature's legs, cutting at its tendons and trying to do as much damage as possible.

I sent another blast of fire at it, aimed at its eyes, and to keep it from turning around to attack Dart and Silas.

The creature refocused on me and the crystal in my hand, snarled, and roared again right before it charged me.

"Shit," I yelped and started to run away, but the creature was faster.

"Nadia!" Silas yelled.

"No!" Dart bellowed.

I turned to see what they were yelling about.

A huge red tongue slammed into me as the monster grabbed me in its slobbery mouth and swallowed me.

13

"Did you just get eaten?" Norma asked softly.

"I'm about to," I groaned as I hung with one hand onto a bone stuck between two of the goat's fangs.

I wanted to let go of the crystal or put it in my pocket, but Loki had told me not to let go of it.

Saliva soaked my clothes, body, and, most grossly, my face.

"I'm going to need ten showers after this," I grumbled.

The creature's throat kept convulsing as it tried to swallow me, but I hung on for all I was worth, refusing to be swallowed. I had no idea what its stomach held, but being burned alive by stomach acid didn't sound like a fun way to die.

"You're not going to die as long as you hold on to that crystal," Norma reminded me. *"Loki wouldn't kill you now that his grandsons are infatuated with you."*

"I hope you're right," I whispered.

The goat demon creature thing stumbled sideways and the bone started to dislodge from tis tooth.

"Crap. Crap. Crap," I chanted as I prayed it would hold.

"Even if I released your full powers, could you get out?" Norma asked.

"I don't know!" I snapped. "Your demonic wings won't be able to expand in here, so I can't fly out. Sure, I could pull my sword, but I'd draw it while we fell down its throat and I don't know if I could cut it open before I reached the stomach acid."

"You're hopeless," the useless demon holding my powers hostage grumbled.

"Loki," I growled. "I hope you really do love your grandsons because I want to wring your damn neck right now!"

"Threatening a god doesn't seem like a good idea right now," Norma whispered.

"I'm going to do whatever I can to keep myself alive right now," I snapped. "It would be great if someone helped me get out of this."

"You could help yourself out of this if you tried a little," Norma grumbled.

"I swear, I'm going to cut your horns off if I ever see you in person," I threatened her.

She made a purring sound. *"Promises. Promises."*

I laughed despite the circumstances. That was one of her charms, she could make me laugh even when I was bleeding. It was a big reason why I wasn't looking for a way to get rid of her or our contract yet.

"Options?" I asked as we swayed back and forth with my hold on the bone.

"Hope one of those two outside can save us, call for Thor or Loki, let go and see what happens," she said.

"Cool," I whispered. "All terrible options."

She chuckled, but said nothing.

The creature listed sideways and then fell so hard the bone was dislodged. Thankfully, we were on our side and didn't get swallowed.

"*Hurry!*" she snapped, like I wasn't already trying to crawl out of its mouth.

I made it out of the creature's mouth just before it snapped its jaws closed and stood upright, eyes fixed back on me.

"Nadia!" Dart yelled, ran to me, picked me up in his arms, and ran as fast as he could away. "You're alive. Oh, thank the gods. You're alive."

"Dart," I whispered, "you're covered in spit now."

"I'll get covered in anything to keep you safe," he whispered.

Unsure how to respond, I remained silent.

He set me down on a grassy hill, pulled a weird looking crocheted doll from his bag, and tapped me on the forehead with the doll.

Immediately, all of the spit and stuff disappeared off of me and I felt clean again.

"Whoa," I whispered.

He put the doll away and looked back towards the goat that Silas was keeping busy. "We damaged it, but it's still got a lot of health left."

"Any idea what truly hurts it?" I asked as I stood and dusted off my clothes.

"Were you damaging it inside?" he asked.

I shook my head. "I was holding onto a bone stuck in its

tooth and this at the same time." I held up the crystal to remind him.

He scowled. "I'm wondering if it's a time limit thing. Like, we have to wait until the sun rises and then it will be at its weakest."

"Can you two hold out that long?" I asked. "I have a terrible feeling it's going to try to eat me and the crystal again."

He scowled. "I won't let that happen ever again."

"Dart," I whispered and set my hand on his shoulder, "it's okay. I'm fine."

He set his hand atop mine and said, "Let's help Silas. If we can have you swap between sides, we can alternate attacks and try to kill it before it even has a chance to attack you again."

"I could fly," I offered softly.

He frowned and looked at me. "Fly?"

"When the demon lets my full powers out, I have wings," I explained.

"Yes, fly as high as you can to get out of its reach, even its jump, and keep it distracted," he ordered me.

I nodded and Norma let out more powers so I could release my wings and fly up into the air above the goat demon. I flew high enough that even if it jumped it wouldn't reach me. "Hey, ugly!" I yelled at it. "Bet you're still hungry, aren't you?" I taunted and waved the crystal at it.

It roared, jumped, and its teeth snapped a few inches short of my toes.

"Okay, higher it is," I grumbled and flew higher up into

the air. I did not want to lose my legs or feet because I didn't fly high enough into the air.

"*Higher,*" Norma ordered me without explanation.

I obeyed because occasionally, she provided good intel.

Higher and higher I went, until I was a dozen or so feet out of reach of its claws, even if it decided to jump.

Dart and Silas still attacked it, doing a lot of damage judging by the amount of blood that coated the ground.

I moved backwards, drawing it away from the blood-slicked ground so Dart and Silas wouldn't slip.

Silas was coated in magic, his eyes glowed an eerie silver, and he kept using magic spells that didn't look familiar to me.

"*He's given into the magic,*" Norma whispered. "*It might be hard to call him back from that.*"

"Silas knows what he's doing," I said with certainty. "He's been in this guild and doing missions for a decade." He was one of the youngest to be admitted to a guild.

"*I'm telling you that he's not himself right now. Watch out for him and make sure once the creature is down that he doesn't go for Dart next.*"

That statement had me more worried than I wanted to admit.

I thought back to Loki's words and scowled. "He told me to hold on to it until I saw the guys. I don't think I'm going to be able to let go even after we kill the creature."

She chuckled. "*You just now realized that?*"

The goat creature had a horned and scaled tail and it swung it right into Dart, sending him flying into a tree. His impact made a sickening crack and when he slid down, he didn't get up.

"Dart!" I screamed.

Silas began chanting, held his palms facing each other, and moved them together until they created a triangle.

"*Get Dart!*" Norma screamed.

Without question, I flew down, scooped Dart up into my arms, and flew back up into the air, even higher than I had been before.

The goat tried to bite me, snapping its jaws as I flew by it, but thankfully missed.

Silas screamed the last word of the chant and black light exploded from his hands and hit the goat.

The goat screamed in pain, thrashing back and forth as the light surrounded it.

Silas smiled and threw back his head as he laughed in a strange voice, very unlike his.

"Dart," I whispered, eyes focused on the goat and Silas. "Please wake up."

"I'm awake," he slurred.

"Something's off with Silas," I whispered.

"What else is new?" he whispered and groaned. "I feel like I got hit and run over by a cart."

"Close, the goat smacked you into a tree," I explained.

"That explains the headache," he said and rubbed at the back of his head. "Why are you holding me, though?"

"The demon told me to grab you once Silas started using weird magic. I don't question her in matters like that, she knows more than me and I assumed it meant you would be in trouble if you were too close to him when the magic was used," I explained.

"Okay, do you have any ideas?"

I shook my head as I watched Silas jump onto the back

of the goat creature and start stabbing it with a sword. Was it wrong to admit I was totally turned on watching it?

"*Not at all,*" Norma purred.

"No," I answered both.

"He does look different," Dart said.

The goat's tail grew longer and thinner, it used the new tail to grab Silas and throw him away from it. As if that weren't bad enough, it suddenly sprouted wings, and launched into the air right at me.

"Run!" I screamed at Dart, dropped him onto the back of the goat creature so he could springboard off of it, and turned to flee.

The goat snapped its teeth around my ankle, successfully catching me in its mouth.

I screamed in pain and tried to use my fire magic around its mouth to force it to release me, but it held tight.

"Nadia!" three familiar male voices yelled.

Jasper, Grayson, and Parker ran towards us, their bodies enlarging as they moved.

"How did they find me?" I asked as I moved closer to the goat's mouth, trying to move my ankle out of its teeth, but each movement caused excruciating pain that made me scream.

"*Loki,*" Norma whispered.

Right, the crystal.

14

Jasper ran forward, grabbed the goat's top and bottom jaw, and pulled, his biceps flexing as he used his giant stature and power to open it.

As soon as there was enough room for me to get free, I flew away.

My flight was short-lived as the pain from my definitely broken ankle had me floundering and falling towards the ground.

Grayson caught me and tucked me against his chest. "Status?"

"Broken ankle," I panted.

"You're almost out of magic, too," he whispered. "Let it go. I've got you."

The goat's head appeared, mouth agape, and headed straight towards us.

"Gray!" I screamed and tucked into a small ball in his hands.

He jumped to the side, rolled on the ground, and stood

back up. The entire time, he had kept me protected against his chest. "Bastard."

"Trickster made me hold this," I whispered and waved the crystal at him. "Said I had to hold onto it until I saw you again or I'd die."

His eyes widened and his mouth dropped open as he looked at the crystal. He turned and yelled, "Parker! She's got it!"

Parker ran over to me, body thrumming with fury. "Give it," he ordered me.

"But—"

He didn't wait, just took it from my hand, ran over to the goat, and slammed it into the goat's right eye.

The goat screamed, pink smoke billowed out of the eye socket, and it fell to the ground, unmoving.

Parker pulled the crystal out, wiped it off on his pants, and put it in his pocket.

"Give her to me!" Silas bellowed.

Grayson turned towards Silas who was still glowing and covered in the black smoke. "Easy, mate. She's injured."

Silas snarled and growled. "Give her. To me."

"Just do it," I whispered to Grayson.

"He's not in his right mind," Grayson whispered.

"Do it," Jasper ordered him. "He's too far gone and I don't want to hurt him."

Grayson reluctantly set me on my feet – well, foot – since I couldn't put pressure on the broken one.

Silas's black smoke surged forward, covering me and blocking out the rest of the world.

I could hear the brothers yelling, but within the smoke, I could not move.

"You're an interesting creature," a deep voice I'd never heard before said. "I can see why he likes you."

"Who are you?" I asked.

"I am the darkness, the night, the fear, the thing that goes bump in the night," he replied, his voice moving around me in a slow circle.

"Are you trying to intimidate me?" I asked with a smirk.

"You don't scare easily, which is exactly what *he* needs," he said. "He needs someone who can accept his darkness."

"He? As in Silas?" I asked for clarification.

"Did you know that he dreamt of you before you came?" he asked.

Silas had dreamed of me?

"I do hope you live up to the expectations."

"Show yourself," I ordered and raised my chin defiantly.

"Oh, honey, you aren't yet ready for that. For now, just know that this smoke won't harm you. Anyone else, including the shifty boy you brought with you, it will destroy. You …" He chuckled. "You can embrace this smoke with open arms."

"Why?"

"Because you are meant to join him."

"Him? Silas?" I asked with a scowl.

"I'll return him to normal, but he will be weakened. Protect him or I shall tear you apart piece by piece."

With that warning, the smoke disappeared and Silas fell into my chest, causing me to fall to my butt with him in my lap, sound asleep.

Dart stood with the trio, all scowling as they looked at me and the sleeping Silas.

"So, I think I met a god just now," I said with a smile and set my hand on Silas's head. "You all look worried."

"We thought you were dead," Parker admitted and sank to his knees with a sigh.

Everyone else sat down with wearied groans and exhales.

"I'm not so easily killed, thank you very much," I scoffed.

"That smoke burns, but you look fine," Dart commented and moved closer to me.

I held out my hand to him, letting him touch my arm. "I'm fine, Dart. The smoke didn't hurt me. If the voice I heard is to be believed, it won't ever hurt me."

"The voice?" Grayson asked.

"Not my story to tell." I shook my head, looking down at Silas. My brows furrowed as I thought about the dream the being had mentioned. What was this dream? Why hadn't Silas mentioned it?

"Why are you all here anyway?" Dart asked. "Now that I'm not freaking out thinking she's going to be eaten alive or destroyed, I'd like some answers."

"We were on a mission, far from here, looking in a very old dungeon where the fabled Crystal of Souls was hidden," Grayson explained. "The crystal was rumored to hold the power to control demons and was our goal."

"We made it past all of the traps and into the treasure room," Parker continued. "Yet the center pedestal where the crystal was supposed to be was empty."

"Grandfather came to us and explained that a crafty little girl had stolen it, using it to resurrect a beast to devour the souls of those who had tormented her and those who had allowed her torment to occur," Jasper said.

My eyes widened. "It wasn't me!"

They all smiled.

Dart scowled. "The girl who called us, the one who submitted the request. It was her, wasn't it?"

"We can't confirm that yet, but we're fairly certain," Grayson said with a nod.

My brows furrowed. "Wait, does that mean the goat has been eating the men who assaulted her?" A huge knot formed in my stomach and I felt like throwing up. She had gone into that dungeon, gotten the crystal, summoned the goat, all to kill the man, or men, who had been assaulting her, and kill the ones who allowed it to happen.

It made me want to find them and kill them all over again.

"Unfortunately, the demon didn't want to stop once it killed them. Well, that's my assumption," Grayson said with a shrug.

"You're right," a small female voice said behind us.

Carefully, I scooted Silas's head off my lap and stood to face her.

She cowered at the tree line, her body shaking as she hugged herself. "Their attacks didn't stop and … I had to do *something*. The demon didn't stop after killing the ones I ordered it to, though. I didn't mean to … I just wanted them to stop. I wanted it to stop … the pain. I wanted the pain to stop."

I walked to her and pulled her into a hug. "It's all over, sweetheart. They're all dead and can't hurt you or anyone else again."

She cried as she clung to me.

The fury within my soul burned bright. These people had hurt this child and done unspeakable things to her. I didn't blame her for turning to a demon for help.

I had done the same.

"Will you turn me in?" she asked.

Before anyone else could respond, I did. "Absolutely not."

She sagged against me. "Thank you. Thank you."

"I wish I could have done more," I whispered honestly.

She cried more and I continued to hug her.

Silas woke up after an hour of napping on my lap. When he realized where he was, he leapt to his feet and walked to the trees without glancing back.

He obviously needed some time, so I stayed sitting on the ground.

The girl went back to her village, telling them how we'd saved them and that the threat was over.

The guys all agreed to keep her secret, mostly due to my puppy eyes it seemed, but she deserved this bit of closure. She deserved her vengeance.

"In two days," Grayson asked, "are you available for a date?"

I played with the end of my hair and acted like I didn't care. "Possibly."

Parker smirked. "Promise there won't be any giants trying to attack us this time."

I sighed dramatically. "Well, now I'm not interested at all."

"Seriously, please come out with us," Jasper said. "We'll even pick you up at your guild."

"Aren't you worried about your mom?" I asked. "She really hates my guts and she'll probably smite me before letting me get serious with you guys."

"Let me handle my daughter," Loki said as he appeared beside Parker.

Parker turned and punched Loki's shoulder. "You're a bastard."

Loki rubbed his shoulder and said, "Everyone's alive and you got a chance to see Nadia again. I think I'm an incredibly helpful and supportive grandfather."

"Meddlesome," I muttered without looking at him.

"Maybe we should just talk to her ourselves," Parker suggested.

Loki shook his head. "Don't approach your mother about Nadia until you're ready to claim her. Trust me, that's the only time you should discuss Nadia with her."

Claim me? What the crap did that mean?

With a wink in my direction, he disappeared.

Gods were such pains in my ass!

15

Once we returned to the guild, Silas hid in his room for several days, refusing to come out for even Paolo. There was no doubt that he was hiding from me, which made me sad.

I thought that perhaps the experience would help him open up to me, explain what the being had said, but obviously that wasn't going to happen.

As promised, the trio came to the guild to pick me up for our date.

Dart walked out front with me, but instead of trying to intimidate them or being rude, he bumped fists with them and told them to have fun. He noticed my wide eyes and smirked. "I'm not blind, Nadia. You guys fit together really well. Plus, I've seen that they're more than capable of protecting you. My only concern when you leave is your safety and I know they'll take it just as seriously as I would."

I gave him a hard hug and kissed his cheek. "I'm so glad we became partners."

He pushed me towards the trio of brothers and said, "You be nice to them."

The curtain in Silas's room moved, catching both Dart's and my eyes.

"He might come out once I leave the grounds," I whispered. "Try to make him understand that nothing's changed between us, please?"

Dart squeezed my shoulder and nodded once. "Will do. Now, go forget the seriousness and have a good night. Send a message if you need me to pick you up."

I smiled wide, waved, and jogged down the steps to the trio.

"Ready?" Parker asked.

"Yep!" I replied eagerly with a wide smile.

Parker led the way while Jasper and Grayson walked beside me.

If I wanted to hold their hand, did I have to choose between them? If I chose, would the others get jealous and get upset? I really wasn't sure how this type of relationship worked. I knew there were lots of multi-partner relationships, but I'd never been around them long enough to witness any of this.

"Why are you scowling so much? You look like you're thinking about something pretty serious," Jasper commented.

Heat bloomed on my cheeks as embarrassment coursed through me. "Um, nothing. So, how have you guys been the past couple of days? Do anything exciting?"

Grayson shook his head. "We were super lazy the last few days. Just playing games and relaxing."

"Relaxing is good after a serious mission," I said. "I'm sure it was needed."

"Then Mom summoned us and made us do a ton of chores around her place," Jasper said.

I flinched. "Did … anything else happen while you were there?"

Jasper smiled softly. "She didn't bring you up and per Grandfather's order, we didn't bring you up to her either."

A huge breath I hadn't realized I'd been holding released. "That's good." As much as they said their mom wasn't allowed to interfere with their love lives, I knew a lot of people who ended up separating because their parents didn't approve of their significant others.

The last thing I wanted was to get emotionally invested and *then* have them leave me.

"So, what are we doing tonight?" I asked as we continued to walk.

"First, food, and then fun," Grayson answered.

"What type of fun?" Not that I didn't like surprises, but these three were unpredictable.

Parker spun around, walked backwards, winked, and said, "You'll just have to wait to find out."

Rolling my eyes in response was the best answer I could give.

They took me to a restaurant in town I'd never been to before. It was definitely an upper-class type of establishment just judging by the well-dressed staff and fancy linens on the tables.

Grayson pulled out a chair for me and I swallowed nervously. I wasn't used to nice things and I wasn't really certain how to act when they were being gentlemanly.

"Thank you," I said as I sat and he scooted me in.

He dropped a kiss on my cheek before taking his seat next to me. "You're welcome."

"I take it you've eaten here before?" I asked as I picked up the menu before me.

"We love it here. They have the best food in the city," Grayson answered.

"We don't come often, just once in a while as a treat when we've completed a difficult mission or task and a few times with friends," Jasper added.

When I saw the prices on the menu, I almost fled. It was too expensive!

"You know, I'm suddenly not feeling very hungry," I whispered and took a big gulp of water from the glass on the table.

"We owe you for your help on the demon mission," Parker said. "Please, order whatever you want from the menu."

Even with that offer, I didn't want to order much. I could always snack when I got back to the guild.

"Are you ready to order?" a waiter dressed in an expensive gray suit asked as he came over with his hands clasped behind him. A pad of paper and a pen made from a feather floated in the air beside his shoulder.

"I'll have a chicken salad," I said with a smile.

The pen wrote the order down on the pad of paper while the waiter continued to look at me. "To drink?" he asked.

"Just water," I said and took another drink to emphasis the point.

Grayson whispered something to Jasper who frowned and nodded once.

"Is that all, miss?" the waiter asked, forcing me to stop staring at Jasper and Grayson.

I looked up and smiled. "Yes."

He turned to the guys and took their orders. Each ordered what seemed like two meals and a bunch of appetizers.

After the waiter left, the guys turned their attention back to me.

"So, any missions planned?" I asked when no one spoke for a minute.

Grayson nodded. "We just picked one today."

"Having a fourth would make it easier," Jasper said with a smile.

Working with them would be fun.

I shook my head while smiling. "Sorry, but I have partners already, remember?"

"It'd just be one mission," Parker said and gave me big eyes.

"Sorry, boys. If you want to spend more time with me, you'll just have to ask me out on more dates."

"What about a trip?" Grayson asked.

"A trip?" No one had ever asked me to go on a trip before.

"Yeah, just an overnight trip to go play in the snow," Parker said. "Sledding, snowball fights, and snowman building contests."

"Do you do this often?" It sounded like they did this frequently.

"Twice a year," Jasper said with a nod.

"I've actually never been to the snow before. When would we go?" I'd have to advise the guild and get their approval.

"In four days," Jasper answered.

Four days?

"That's pretty soon," I said, and gnawed on my lower lip. Would that be enough time to mend things with Silas and also make him relax about me going?

Dart seemed more at ease with the guys and likely wouldn't try to convince me to stay.

"Think about it," Grayson said. "We'd love for you to come."

"Just us four?"

They all nodded.

The waiter and two additional staff came to our table carrying trays with all of the food that we'd ordered.

The guys pushed the food into the middle and looked at me and my little salad.

"Can we get a couple extra plates?" Grayson requested. "We'd like to share our food."

The waiter nodded, walked to a cupboard nearby, and brought back several plates.

"Take some of whatever you want," Grayson said to me with a wide smile.

I hesitated for a moment, but I could never turn down free food.

Filling up one of the plates with a little bit of every-thing, I hadn't realized how hungry I was until I started eating. I had completely cleaned my plate and had started to add more when I realized they were looking at me.

I hesitated, but Parker pushed one of the bowls of chicken wings towards me. "Take as much as you want."

"I've already eaten a lot," I said, embarrassed.

"Waiter," Parker called.

"Yes?" he asked.

"Can we get another two orders of the wings. They're the best."

The waiter ran off to place the order.

Parker took my plate, put a lot of additional food on it, and handed it back to me.

I waited until they added more to their plates before I started eating again.

The food was so delicious. I understood why they came here as often as they could.

My stomach still wasn't full, but I stopped eating and pushed my plates forward. "That was delicious." I placed my hands on my stomach to reiterate that fact.

They scowled a moment, filled their plates up more, and resumed eating.

After we all finished eating, they stood and Grayson held out his hand to me. "On to the fun."

His green eyes held mischief in them that reminded me of Loki.

I set my hand in his and smiled. "Let's go."

We headed out of the restaurant and I noticed more than a few women staring, which made me want to preen, but I didn't.

Outside, the cool night air surrounded me and I drew in a deep breath.

16

Parker and Jasper joined us a moment later and walked behind us.

People talked and laughed together as we passed and I felt genuinely free for the first time in a long time. Well, not completely free since Norma was still in me, but free enough.

Grayson led me to a saloon that had drinks and shows. I had always wanted to come here, but with money so tight, it had always been a pipe dream.

Parker pushed open the door and kissed my cheek as I stepped by him, making my cheeks heat.

Inside, a woman in a ruffled dress that hung to her knees greeted us. "Evening. Table for four?"

"Yes, ma'am," Grayson said.

The room had a bar on the right side, a stage on the farthest wall, and tables with chairs in the middle.

There were dozens of circular tables, most just big enough for two people to sit at, but some large enough for four. Most of the tables were filled and we managed to snag the last four-person table.

"I'll get the drinks, what would you like?" Parker asked.

I shrugged. "Something tasty." The truth was that I hadn't drank much so I didn't know what to even ask for.

He winked and walked over to the bar.

"Have you ever been here before?" Jasper asked.

I shook my head, unable to keep the smile off my face. "I've always wanted to come."

The stage was wooden, with thick, red velvet drapes lined in gold-laced trim. There were a few fairy lanterns, lanterns powered by magic, providing dim lighting to the stage, but I didn't see any spotlights or other equipment. Did they hide it until the people walked on?

"You're in for a treat tonight then," Jasper said. "Veluptua is the best."

She was infamous for her amazing voice and dance moves. Tickets to her show were usually sold out months ahead of time.

"How did you guys score tickets?" I asked. "Don't they sell out really fast?"

Grayson leaned over and whispered, "We have our ways, beautiful."

Beautiful?

"Your drink, milady," Parker said, setting a glass of bright pink liquid in front of me.

As the liquid swirled within the glass, sparkles shone in the lights. Picking the small glass up carefully, I sniffed.

Strawberries and a hint of citrus.

Deciding there was no time like the present, I took a

drink and a burst of flavor shot across my tongue and the image of a strawberry field overtook me.

"Whoa," I whispered as the image faded and I came back to reality.

"You'll want to drink that slow ..." Parker said, but I'd already chugged half of it.

"So good!" I gasped and licked my lips.

"Oh, boy," Jasper whispered. "We're going to want to stick close to her the rest of the night."

A tall, voluptuous woman sashayed out onto the stage to whistles and cheers. My eyes fixed on her and I couldn't look away, even though I felt one of the guys drape his arm around my shoulders and felt a hand on my leg. "Are there any virgins here?" she asked. "Anyone who has never seen me before?"

My hand shot into the air before I even registered the questions.

She smirked as she looked at me. "Hello, doll. Aren't you a lovely thing, and surrounded by such juicy morsels? What's your name?"

"Nadia," I answered.

"Nadia, tonight I dedicate my songs to you." She winked, the lights went out, the room turned completely pitch black, and someone started playing on a piano.

She let out a note that had my spine straightening and me jerking upright in the chair, causing the arm across my shoulders to fall down.

For the next three minutes, my eyes were glued to her as she sung about love, lust, and passion, the feelings echoing deep within my soul. Had I been able to move, I would have fanned myself.

When the song finished, I stood and clapped as loud as I could.

She winked at me and walked to a stool where a glass of liquid sat, taking a long drink from it.

I took a drink from mine, but ended up finishing it.

Before the guys could talk to me, she started another song and once again, I was mesmerized; the words she spoke were like she plucked them from my past and put them into song. The pain, the loneliness, the vast emptiness within me that not even Norma filled, the desire to be loved and wanted. She articulated what I could never say on my own. Never explain to people like Thor, who had never gone without.

This time when her song ended, I felt everyone's eyes on me.

My cheeks were warm, but I wasn't crying or anything, so why were they looking at me?

"You're glowing," Grayson whispered and twirled a piece of my rainbow hair. "Wow."

Veluptua jumped down from the stage, marched to me, and said, "You must leave."

"What?" I asked, confused and uncertain.

She looked at Jasper, Grayson, and Parker. "Get her out of here. Now!"

The doors burst open and three men in black suits walked in, their eyes solid black.

Veluptua took my hands and smiled. "You are going to do incredible things; I can sense it. And these men ... they are going to help you. They are your missing pieces, your soulmates. Do not let them go."

For a moment, I thought she meant the men in suits,

but when she stepped between us and the men, I realized she meant the brothers.

"You are not welcome here," she snapped, as magic swirled around her in a vortex, forcing them to step back.

"Give us the soulless one."

My brows furrowed. Were they talking about me?

"She is not soulless. You misread what was spoken tonight and what was exposed. Leave this place now or I will take it as an attack." Her body glowed and she started to hover above the ground.

Jasper gripped my hand and pulled me away from Veluptua and out a side door that led into an alley.

Before I could ask what was going on, Hel stepped out of the shadows, pressed two fingers to my forehead, and I fainted.

17

"Mom, you can't be serious!" Jasper snapped.

"She's going to get you three killed!" Hel yelled.

I groaned and pressed a hand to my head. It felt like I'd been run over by a cart.

"Take it slow," Grayson said, his warm hands slide along my back and helped me sit up fully.

"She's been a burden on our lives since Thor found her," Hel snapped. "Just send her back and stop seeing her. It's not that much to ask. She is only using you and tricking you as well."

"I never tricked anyone," I whispered. "I was a child, and neither Thor nor I realized the ramifications of that contract when he signed it. I have offered, dozens of times, to cancel the contract, but *he* is the one who refuses." Reluctantly, I opened my eyes and looked at Hel.

She was glorious, glowing, and looked ready to kill me.

Grayson tilted my chin up so I had to look into his eyes. "What hurts?"

"My head hurts the most, but my entire body feels like I got run over," I admitted.

Hel scoffed and folded her arms across her chest.

"Have you ever asked Thor about the contract? Why he won't break it? You know that I'm just a human and not capable of forcing anyone, god or demigod, to do anything against their will. Have you ever considered why you hate a child so much? A child who only ever admired you for being a strong and independent woman."

Hel's eyes widened, but she said nothing.

Angrboda stepped through the door and snapped at Hel, "What is wrong with you?"

"M-Mom?" Hel asked and her arms dropped to her side. "What are you doing here?"

"I called her," Parker said. "You won't listen to us, so maybe you will listen to grandma."

Angrboda walked over to the couch I sat on, sat beside me, and pressed her hand to my head. Her scowl deepened. "You tried to use *that* spell on her? Are you mad? Do you want to drive your sons away?"

Hel scoffed. "She's no one to them. You think—"

"She is *not* no one," Grayson snapped.

"How do you even know her?" Hel asked, her eyes narrowing. She glared at me. "Did you sink your dirty little claws into my mother, too?"

"Your sons brought her to meet me," Angrboda said.

Hel's eyes widened and she looked between her three boys. "Y-You brought her to meet your grandma?"

They nodded.

"What is going on?" Loki demanded as he walked in and straight up to Hel. "Thor is flipping his shit claiming that Nadia—" he stopped talking when he saw me. A huge sigh escaped him. "Dammit, Hel."

"You knew they were dating her?" Hel's mouth dropped open.

"I always keep tabs on my family," Loki said. He walked over to me and Angrboda. "What's wrong with her? Why is she in pain?"

"Hel tried to use *that* spell on her," Angrboda said.

Loki spun and green energy sparked around him. "Hel, explain yourself."

For the first time, Hel looked nervous and cowed. "She was tricking them. Using her—"

"You are so blind that I can't even believe you can see me. How many fingers am I holding up?" He held up two fingers and quickly dropped them. "Never mind. Nadia, come with me so we can ease Thor and your guild's worry. They've been frantically searching for you because they can't sense you here."

"Where is … here?" I asked.

"Underworld," Grayson answered.

That partially explained the massive headache. Humans weren't supposed to survive here.

"Your demon has proven lucky for you once again," Angrboda said with a wink. "If she weren't inside of you, you might be dead right now."

Strangely, I couldn't really feel Norma right now and she was eerily silent.

"Don't worry, she's just busy protecting you," Angrboda whispered when she saw my expression shift.

Grayson picked me up in his arms and snarled at his mother.

"We're leaving," Jasper said as he came to stand beside us.

"She's not worthy of you three," Hel snapped, finally coming back to her senses.

"I'm not," I agreed.

Grayson clicked his tongue.

"You don't get a say in who we date or who we decide to take as a wife," Parker said softly. "Stay out of our love lives, Mother."

"Thank you for coming," I whispered to Angrboda.

She patted my cheek. "Forgive her, she is just an overprotective mother."

I smiled and nodded once.

Loki set his hand on Grayson's shoulder and Jasper and Parker set their hands on Loki's shoulders. "Think about what this could have cost you," Loki said to Hel.

Hel's eyes widened, she looked at me, and fire flared in her eyes.

Great, now she hated me even more and I hadn't even done anything wrong.

Loki teleported us right onto Golden Alicorn grounds, in the field in front of the main house.

Thor, Dart, and Paolo were together talking and Silas stood off to the side, his hands balled into fists.

"I've returned Nadia," Loki said. "You can call off the war." He said it jokingly, but the lightning crackling in the sky showed just how upset Thor was.

Thor marched towards me, but Silas was the one who reached us first.

Silas's fist connected with Grayson's jaw before I even realized what was happening.

Parker and Jasper stepped forward, but Grayson shook his head once.

"Silas, I'm fine," I said quickly.

The dark smoke was in his eyes and starting to seep out around his feet. "If you cannot protect her from your own family, do not involve her in your lives," Silas snapped.

Grayson set me on my feet, but kept an arm around my waist. "We know we must atone with Nadia over this. Once we realized what was happening, we called in reinforcements."

"They mean me," Loki whispered loudly.

I rolled my eyes, certain they meant Angrboda.

"We never would have let Mother kill her," Jasper said. "We would sacrifice ourselves before we let that happen."

"If a member of my guild is hurt due to your neglect again, I won't hesitate," Silas said.

He was so mad that the words barely made it out of his mouth, his jaw clenched so tightly that his skin was white where the the muscles strained.

I patted Grayson's arm, the one still wrapped around my waist, and he reluctantly released me. Taking a step forward, I hugged Silas. "Thank you, for caring."

His tense body froze and then he completely relaxed and hugged me tenderly. "I thought you were dead. All I heard was Thor say you were in the Underworld."

The black smoke swirled around us, but in a strange ... caressing manner.

"I'm safe," I said, since it was the only thing important right now.

Snapping back into himself, he stepped back and the

smoke disappeared. He cleared his throat and said, "I'm glad you're back."

"We need to talk later," I told him. "First, let me say bye."

Spinning on my heels, I walked up to Dart and as soon as I raised my arms, he threw himself forward to hug me. "I knew you couldn't be dead. I could still feel you, sense you. I thought Thor had to be wrong."

I patted his back and smiled up at him. "Technically, Thor was right. I was in the Underworld, just not dead."

Thor's patience ran out and he grabbed me to hug me. "I was so worried," he whispered. "I felt you go into the Underworld and lost it."

"He destroyed a forest," Loki muttered.

"I'm sore, but alive," I said.

He scowled down at me. "What spell did she try to use on you?"

I turned my head to look at Loki. "Yeah, what spell were you and Angrboda talking about?"

Loki put his hands in his pockets, looked up at the sky, whistled, and rocked back and forth on his heels.

My eyes narrowed, but there was nothing I could do to force him to talk.

"Well, it doesn't matter what she tried, because it didn't work," I said with a bright smile up at Thor.

He set his hand on my cheek and said, "I failed to keep you safe. Does this void our contract?"

My brows furrowed. "I-I don't think so." Reaching up, I rubbed my head, which was still hurting.

Thor looked over my head. "Can you heal her?"

"Ask nicely," Loki said.

Thor's eyes narrowed. "Please heal her."

Loki walked over, set his fingers on my head, and beamed. "See? That wasn't that hard."

"That's what she said," I said with a wry smile as I glanced up at Loki.

He threw his head back as he laughed, continuing to heal me. "I see why my grandsons are enamored with you."

I remembered what Voluptua had said and glanced over at the trio, who were talking quietly to Dart.

Were they my soulmates? I hadn't even thought that was a true thing.

"Something happened before Hel got you, didn't it?" Loki asked in a soft whisper.

I nodded once. "Ask them and maybe give me some intel based on what they say?" I requested and smirked up at him.

He tapped the tip of my nose. "Sorry, family first."

The pain disappeared from my body and I stretched my arms. "Thank you. I feel much better."

"Norma?" I asked mentally.

No response.

"She's still there," Loki said. "Angrboda is right, she saved you. She's probably just recuperating. Give her a day."

"My powers," I whispered. "Does that mean ..." Palm out, I tried to summon fire, but nothing happened.

Loki placed a hand on my shoulder. "Looks like you're grounded for a little bit."

"How long?" I asked, my voice weak.

"A day or two." He gave a shrug of his shoulder. Raising his voice so the others could hear, he said, "My boys can stay with you to protect you if you—"

"They can't stay here," Silas snapped. "This is Golden Alicorn property."

"It's fine," I said, and turned to Paolo. Bowing I said, "I'm sorry for worrying you."

"I'm just glad you're alive and well," Paolo said. "Come on, Silas. Let's leave her to say goodbye."

Silas wanted to object, but he followed Paolo after one more glare at the brothers.

Dart squeezed one of my shoulders as he walked by and into the house.

Loki winked and disappeared, forcing Thor to leave with him.

18

I walked up to the brothers and smiled. "So, when's our next date? Are all of our dates going to be as exciting?"

Their scowls finally lifted as they smiled or smirked at my questions.

Grayson's scowl quickly returned. "We should be groveling at your feet after our mother—"

"You don't need to apologize. She blindsided all of us outside of the bar. By the way, do you three know who those guys in suits were? Or what they wanted with me?"

"We plan to go back and talk to Voluptua about it tonight," Parker said. "We aren't quite sure why they called you soulless."

"Yeah, that wasn't very nice," I said.

"About what else Voluptua said," Jasper whispered and stepped forward. He rested his hand on my cheek and rubbed his thumb over the bone. "Don't put too much stock in it. We want to develop this relationship because we like you, not because of anything else. Plus, she often tells people what they want to hear."

I flinched, feeling like he was calling me out, and forced his hand to drop away from my face. "Um, right, yeah. I don't really believe in that stuff anyway."

"When can we see you again?" Grayson asked. He stepped forward and his red hair shone in the early morning light.

Morning? How had I not realized that it was already the following day?

"Well, I guess I can't leave the grounds until my magic returns, so in a couple of days at least, according to Loki."

"Are you still willing to go on the trip with us?" Parker asked.

"I do want to go on the trip, but I'm worried about not having magic. If it doesn't come back, I may need to stay here instead," I said.

Parker's brows furrowed and he nodded. "Okay."

"Can we come see you the day we're leaving for the trip, to pick you up or at least see you before we go?" Grayson asked.

"Sure," I agreed with a nod.

"We have something for you," Parker said. "We were going to give it to you after the show, but … well, you know." He pulled out a necklace that had a runic symbol I had never seen before etched into it. "This is our symbol," he explained. "If you hold it in your hand, send a little magic, and call out to us mentally, we'll hear it and can come to you."

They were offering me a permanent way to summon them. That was a … a huge step in our relationship.

"Are … are you sure?" I asked, my voice barely audible.

He set it in the palm of my hand, took my other hand,

and placed it over the top, so I held the necklace between both hands. "Yes."

He kissed me lightly on the lips and stepped back so Grayson could kiss me next.

Jasper brushed my hair over my shoulder and kissed me tentatively. He pulled his lips back, but stayed right in front of me, his breath mixing with mine as he spoke. "I feel like you're upset with me. I don't want to leave, if that's the case."

I gave him a small smile and said, "I know you didn't mean to hurt my feelings, and I'm probably just being ridiculous for even being upset. Don't worry about it. I'll feel better in a bit."

"What did I say?" he asked, frowning. "I—"

I kissed him again and said, "I'll see you in a few days, okay?" Spinning around quickly, before I lost my nerve, I jogged into the house and shut the door behind me with a harsh exhale.

Why did those three make me feel like this?

"You good?" Dart asked with an arched brow.

Heat flooded my face. "Yeah." I pushed off the door and walked to him. "What time is it?"

"Breakfast time," he answered with a scowl, and looked down at me. "No clocks in the Underworld?" His scowl turned into a smile, and I knew he was trying to lighten the mood and make me feel better.

He was definitely the exact person I needed to make it through this life.

I chuckled and shrugged. "Didn't really get a chance to look around."

"Pity," he said, pushing open the door to the dining hall.

Silas wasn't inside, which was fine. I needed to talk to him in private, anyway.

Everyone stared at me, but instead of feeling embarrassed, I walked with my head high to the table we normally sat at.

Dart sat across from me and asked, "How was your date before the craziness?"

"They took me to this fancy restaurant and the food was *so* good," I said. "I wanted to eat all night!"

"We'll have to go there," he said.

I flinched. "It was *pricey*."

"Well, that just means we'll have to make sure we go on a lot of missions before we go. Maybe we can go to celebrate once we have completed our tenth mission?"

"That sounds great," I said with a smile and nod.

After eating and laughing with Dart for an hour, it felt almost like normal again.

I walked to Silas's room and knocked on his door twice.

It took him a few moments to answer, but he reluctantly opened the door.

"Can I come in?" I asked.

He stepped back, giving me room to enter.

His room was dimly lit, the window covered by a black drape, and there were no decorations or pictures. It reminded me of my room.

I sat on top of his dresser and crossed one leg over the other. "I really am okay," I said, smiling.

"You can't access your magic. That's hardly okay," he snapped. He sat down on the edge of his bed and looked down at his hands.

"I spoke to your, the, um, god," I said quickly before I lost my nerve to have this conversation.

His head snapped up; eyes wide. "What?"

"What happened during that mission? Why did you lose control? And how come no one else has ever heard about you having that black smoke power? What is it?" The questions tumbled out of my mouth one after the other, leaving no time for him to answer.

"Slow down," he said with a soft chuckle. He ran a hand through his hair, but it got tangled.

"Your hair must grow super fast, I'm jealous. When's the last time you brushed it?" I asked, grabbing the hair brush that was sitting beside me atop his dresser. I hopped to my feet and walked towards him. The last time I'd seen him, it was only an inch long, how was it so long in just a few days? Did it have to do with the black smoke?

"What? I … I don't know," he admitted, and scrubbed a hand down his face.

Climbing onto his bed behind him, I brushed his hair that was now over four inches long. His shoulders were tense at first, but after a few brushstrokes, they dropped and he exhaled softly.

"You usually keep this shaved, right?" I asked. "Do you want me to shave it?"

He turned, grabbed my wrist to stop my brushing, and said, "I'm sorry. I've been acting like a jerk and I didn't even realize it until it was almost too late."

Too late?

Silas leaned forward and rested his forehead against mine. "I lost it that day when the monster had you. I lost it again when Thor showed up."

"Tell me, please?" I whispered.

"I'm a demigod," he said. "A different one than the trio."

That much was obvious.

"My father is the ruler of the Underworld," he explained. "Well, our Underworld."

"How does that even work?" I asked, and leaned back to see him easier. "How are there multiple Underworlds?"

"I think it depends on your beliefs," Silas said with a shrug. "I'm honestly not sure. I just know that when Thor said you were in the Underworld, I teleported to my father and demanded he give you back to me. However, you weren't there and he told me that you weren't dead … yet."

Of course a god would phrase it that way to get a rise out of his demigod son.

"When I came back …" he rubbed the back of his neck, "… I got into a fight with Thor."

My mouth dropped. "You fought Thor?"

"Yeah, not my best moment. He knew why I was upset and seemed to feel like it was his fault, so he basically let me take my anger out on him."

I would have to thank Thor next time I saw him and make sure he knew that there was nothing he could have done.

"Paolo stopped me and reminded me that if you were in mortal danger, your mark would tell us." He looked at me, meeting my eyes. "We have a problem, and I don't know how to fix it."

"We don't have a problem," I said with a frown. "If I were in your shoes, I might have reacted the same way."

Silas got to his feet and paced across his room. "You don't understand, which is my fault, but I don't know how to make you understand, because I've never been good at this and probably shouldn't even acknowledge it anyway. Acknowledging it could just ruin everything."

I had no idea what he was blabbing about. With a quick step, I moved in his way, forcing him to stop and look at me. "We're partners, right? Just talk to me."

He gripped his hair a moment and then looked into my eyes, wrapped his arms around me, and kissed me.

19

My eyes were closed, yet I could tell that Silas's black smoke was surrounding us. He kissed me and immediately I felt my connection to Norma snap back into place.

We broke apart, both panting, and I stared at him with wide, unbelieving eyes.

"That was not how I expected to get back," Norma said.

"I'm pretty sure I'm in love with you," Silas said. "I feel you and your pain, even more than the brand should have given us. I think … you might be my soulmate."

Was it possible to have multiple soulmates? Because I definitely felt a connection with him, even if I wanted to deny it.

This was going to make things really strange when I saw the trio again.

Oh, shit. The brothers!

I'd just kissed another guy. Well, technically, he had kissed me, but I hadn't pushed him away.

Shit.

I sat on the edge of Silas's bed and stared at his dresser. What was I going to do?

"Nadia?" Silas whispered.

"How do you know soulmates are real?" I asked softly instead of addressing the elephant in the room and letting myself freak out about … everything.

"I asked my father and he said they do exist."

"I … I need to talk to someone who knows about them," I whispered urgently and stood. "Who do we know I can talk to? Would Paolo know? He'll probably know, or know someone I can talk to."

Before I could turn to leave, Silas grabbed my arm to stop me. "Wait, why are you going to talk to him about that?"

"Silas, I can't deny that we have a connection and that I am attracted to you, but someone else told me that I had other soulmates."

"Other?" he asked softly.

"I just need to find out if it is even possible. Things … things are happening so fast. I don't even know which way is up right now."

"I can tell you what's up right now," Norma snickered.

"Shut it."

"I'll come with you," Silas said.

The desire to tell him no was strong, but this did involve him. Should I call the trio to come?

No, Jasper had made it clear he didn't really believe in the soulmates thing, and the last thing I wanted was for them to get into a fight with Silas right now.

Silas released my arm and opened the door to his room.

I walked out and all but ran to Paolo's office.

My hand raised to knock, but the door swung open before I could touch it.

"How can I help you, Nadia?" Paolo asked.

His office was small, just a desk, a few chairs, and a couch.

I walked inside and Silas shut the door behind us. "What do you know about soulmates?"

Paolo smiled. "Oh, this day just got so much more interesting! I knew you were the right choice for this guild."

I sat in the chair in front of his desk and sighed. "Interesting is definitely one of the words people use to describe me."

Paolo raised his hand and the wall to the left spun around, revealing a bookshelf. A book glowed, slid off the shelf, and flew over to his hand. He set it down, flipped a few pages, and held the book out to me.

I set it on the desk so I could read it, and so Silas could read it if he came over, which he immediately did.

"Soulmates do exist, however, there are instances where one person, due to differing circumstances, ends up with more than one. Usually, it has to do with dealing with traumatic childhood experiences severing the soul and sending tiny pieces of their soul into the universe to find their other parts, the ones that can heal that trauma."

"Someone called me soulless the other night," I whispered.

He leaned back and frowned. "You aren't soulless. Shattered, perhaps, but not soulless."

"Where were you that you were called soulless?" Silas asked.

"On our date we went to a show and Voluptua used her powers on me to sing. When she finished, a group of men in suits barged in, saying they wanted the soulless one, which I assumed was me, and Voluptua told them that they misunderstood what had been sung or something like that. The details are a little fuzzy now. She made a comment about me having soulmates and I assumed she meant the trio."

"Is there a test or something you can do to determine the true soulmates?" Silas asked.

Paolo sighed. "I've heard of a spell, but there are rumors that it has adverse side effects, especially if it determines you aren't a soulmate for the caster."

Was it worth the risk? To know for certain if they were your soulmate or not?

"How does a soulmate bond work?" I asked as I resumed reading the book, but so far I hadn't found much helpful information as it was a basic overview.

"That's something I would have to send you to an outside source to discuss." He stood, grabbed a cloak that appeared out of thin air, and a staff that slid out of the top of the desk.

"Can I change first?" I asked. "I've been wearing this since yesterday."

He chuckled. "Right, I forgot that you haven't really had a chance to relax. Go freshen up while I chat with Silas."

As quickly as possible, I showered and changed. I also brushed my teeth and my hair, though I didn't want to waste time braiding it, so I left it in loose waves. Looking in the mirror, I realized that my hair had grown a lot in just the short amount of time that I'd joined this guild. It was down to my butt already. I'd need to cut it soon, or I risked it getting in the way during fights. The last thing I wanted was to be a liability.

"Our connection okay?" I asked Norma aloud as I jogged down the stairs towards Paolo's office.

"*Yes. Almost better than before. Also, it seems like we both leveled up a bit.*"

Gaining more power was always good and helped our end goal.

"Can I come?" Dart asked as he stepped out of the hallway to my right, making me jump sideways.

"Not this time," Silas said.

"I think he should come," I countered as Paolo stepped out of his office. "Dart is our partner and it's important for him to know about his partners' weaknesses."

Silas scowled. "You think … it's a weakness?"

I shrugged one shoulder. "It could be. We don't know for certain."

"Let's go," Paolo ordered and waved his hand, making the front doors of the house open.

"Field trip!" Dart cheered and draped an arm around my shoulders.

"Aren't field trips supposed to be fun?" I countered.

"We just have to make sure we have fun while on it," he said. "We can get into mischief, I'm sure."

"Behave," Paolo threatened.

"That's definitely not how to have fun," Dart countered.

"We should stop by Martha's shop on the way back," Silas said with a mischievous smirk to Dart and me.

Paolo stood up straighter. "Oh, that's a great idea. I haven't been there in a couple of weeks. I'm sure she's missing me by now." Paolo snickered slightly and I saw the tips of his ears turn read.

"Who is Martha?" Dart whispered to Silas.

"Paolo's crush. Apparently, they dated when they were younger, but she opted to open a shop instead of joining a guild, which crushed his heart. She claims it's because she doesn't want to be tied to a guild and take orders from a guild master. She is very powerful and could easily have been a guild master herself."

"This field trip got even more interesting," Dart said. "I'm so glad I'm going."

"She has some of the best items in the country," Paolo boasted and I realized he had been talking the entire time.

I still didn't have much money, so I would just browse and buy things after our next few jobs.

"Oh, uh, I don't need to be grounded anymore," I announced.

Paolo and Dart looked at me.

Palm up, I created a fireball above it. "See?"

Paolo's eyes twinkled as he looked at Silas and back at me. "Curiouser and curiouser."

My face heated and I shook my hand to dissipate the fire.

"That's great!" Dart said.

As we walked through town, many people smiled and waved to Paolo and Silas. Some even came close to walk next to them for a few steps to say something.

What was it like to be so well known? Did they enjoy it?

"I've got this job I've been looking at on the board that I really want to do with you two," Dart said, drawing my attention back to him.

"What is it?" I asked, desperate to talk about anything other than the other topics of interest.

"A group of magically-enhanced beavers keep building dams in the river north of a town and stopping their water supply," Dart said.

Oh, that did sound interesting and fun. "I'm in."

"Me, too," Silas agreed.

"Beavers creep me out," Paolo said and shuddered.

All of us stared at him.

Our guild master … the guild master of the Golden Alicorns, was creeped out by beavers?

"Is it their tails?" Dart asked.

Paolo stopped, spun, mouth open, and asked, "How did you know?"

"Because they are unnatural looking," Dart said.

Dart and Paolo walked side by side, discussing beaver tails, and I just shook my head.

"Platypus, that's a creepy creature," I countered.

"Don't even get me started!" Paolo said.

"Yet chimeras are your favorite creature?" Silas asked Paolo.

"They are a combination, not an abomination. It's different."

Laughter burst out of me as I listened to them discussing different creatures.

"What's the weirdest creature you've seen in person?" Dart asked me.

"I've actually met an alicorn before," I admitted.

"Aren't they majestic?" Paolo asked.

"I rode her, actually. She saved me from a band of cursed wolves. Well, men cursed to be vicious wolves."

"You rode an alicorn?" Paolo gaped. "I chose them as our symbol because they're so majestic and—"

"Amazing," I finished for him. "They really are one of the most graceful and powerful creatures."

"Intelligent, too," Paolo added with a nod.

We walked through town, past all the familiar places I had been, to the housing area, and into a dark alley that smelled like urine and feces with many rats running around.

He knocked on the front door to a small house with wood burning in the fireplace, the smoke billowing out steadily.

"Let me do the speaking," Paolo ordered us.

We nodded our agreement.

A woman in her late fifties, at least, opened the door, her crooked nose the largest part of her face. She looked at us and narrowed her eyes at Paolo. "What do you want?"

"Some of my children need answers that only you can provide. I would like to barter for information on their behalf," Paolo answered. He pulled a dark jewel out of an inner pocket of his cloak and held it out.

She eyed the jewel with extreme interest, licked her lips, looked back at us, and after a brief moment of consideration, stepped back to let us in.

Once the door shut behind us, the entire atmosphere changed. It went from being the dark side of town to being bright, warm, and as though we were in a cottage in the middle of a sunny grass field. She had fresh flowers in vases around the room and some dried flowers hanging on the walls.

The home was lovely, but I dared not voice my thought.

The living room had three couches and two highbacked chairs. Paolo sat in one, so the three of us sat on the middle couch, and as expected, the woman took the other highbacked chair.

She wiggled her fingers.

Paolo set the jewel on the coffee table and it slid along the top before coming to rest right in front of her.

"Ask," she ordered.

"We need information on how soulmate bonds work. More specifically, when someone has more than one," Paolo said quickly.

Her eyes darted to mine and a depthless sadness echoed within her eyes. "You ask much from me, guild master."

"I understand the topic is ... difficult, to discuss, but I would not have come here and bartered so highly if it weren't important." He set a smaller, bright purple jewel, on the table. "Will this be enough?"

She crooked her finger and the bright jewel slid to join the first. With a deep sigh, she nodded once. "Very well."

We settled in our seats now that we all knew we were staying.

"When I was younger," she began, "I had five soulmates."

Five!

"I was stubborn, to say the least," she said. "Having so many mates was unheard of back then. A few of my mates thought I was lying, but it's hard to deny the bond for long."

So many questions burned in my throat, but I held them back, letting her tell her tale.

"I sealed the bond with two of my mates, though it was not purposefully done. We were on a mission and I was injured. They used some of their magic to heal me and the bond solidified. We hadn't realized what we had done until we returned and the bond was visible to others." She raised her eyes to mine. "Once you seal it, a golden thread appears, and is visible for three days. There are ancient texts that describe a celebration being held during that time, to commemorate the bond. Our reception was far from happy. My other mates were livid. They thought I had chosen the two only, and didn't also want them."

That must have been awful. I could only imagine how heartbreaking that must have been for her when she didn't even intentionally seal the bonds.

"There was a guild battle between three guilds, I lived in another country during this time, and those guilds often battled. This battle was long, hard, and many died. One of my mates died before we'd sealed the bond, but I still felt it. Felt the bond snap like a piece of my soul had severed completely off."

Tears sprang to my eyes and Silas set his hand on my knee.

"I ... exploded," she said. "Killed dozens in my rage. When I came to, my guild master kicked me out of the guild and forced me to leave town. My mates left with me, but we were attacked by members of the guild I'd killed. All of them ... all of my mates are dead now."

The silence after those words was almost deafening.

She took a deep breath and looked at me. "How many do you have?"

"I'm not certain," I admitted. "Possibly four."

She looked at Silas. "He's one?"

"We think," I said softly.

"There's one way to tell," she said and looked at Paolo. "Though you may be opposed to it."

"I've heard of the spell and the possible adverse side effects and have advised against it," he said sternly.

"There's another way," she said. "All of the potential mates would need to be in one room, though."

"What is this other way?" Paolo asked, eyes narrowed in suspicion.

"I can't discuss it in front of her, or the suspected one." She stood and waved for Paolo to follow her to the kitchen.

"You sure about this?" Dart asked me. "You could just let things happen, naturally?"

"I'm not sure about anything," I admitted. "I just don't know how to handle this … insanity."

"It is quite crazy," Silas agreed. "Four soulmates?"

"Maybe it's five," Dart teased.

Silas snarled, but ran his hand down his face. "You are a brat."

"I still don't like it," Paolo grumbled as he came back to the room with her behind him. "But it seems like the only way that won't have awful endings." He looked at me. "You have to realize that once you know who you are bound to, it will affect your relationship. If you aren't bound to the brothers …" He trailed off because the implication was there.

If I wasn't bound to them, but I was Silas, I would have to break off my relationship with them.

I didn't want to admit that I was certain about them, more certain than Silas because it was not a logical thing to be certain of.

"What do we have to do?" I asked. "No, wait, what are

the downsides?"

"Depending on how strong they are, they could destroy the area you do this in," she said. "I recommend finding an abandoned town or dead forest."

"We can figure that out later," I said. "I … I don't want to do it yet. I want to wait until after my trip. Until after I talk to them first."

"Trip?" Silas and Dart asked simultaneously.

I nodded. "I'll be gone for two days."

"Where are you going?"

"To their snow cabin," I answered. "I hadn't had a chance to discuss it with you all yet, but with this change, I definitely want to do it before we do use the spell."

Paolo smiled softly. "Approved."

Silas stood and stomped out of the house.

"He won't like it, but you are making a smart decision," the woman said. "Go on the trip and then once you come back, do the spell. I'll be waiting for you."

I gave her a small smile and walked out of the house, Dart at my side.

"Have you been to the snow before?" Dart asked as we walked out.

I shook my head. "I don't think I have warm enough clothes, honestly. I need some better boots."

Dart rocked on his heels. "Let's stop by the store and—"

"Why do you want to go on this trip so much?" Silas asked. "We haven't even gone on one date or anything, and—"

"Silas, I was already dating them and agreed to go on the trip before our talk. If you can't even accept me dating them, we aren't going to work. You have to trust me." I gave him a stern expression and after a moment, his shoulders sagged.

"Fine. Are we ready to go?"

Paolo stepped out and waved us forward, opting to walk behind us this time.

Silas took the lead, which I was glad for, because I wasn't entirely certain I could get us back to the guild without having to make several route changes after getting lost or going the wrong way.

Paolo spoke softly enough that Silas couldn't hear him. "I don't really like this option, but I understand your desire to know for certain."

"I don't want to lead anyone on or cause issues unnecessarily," I whispered. "Plus, the sooner I find this out, the quicker I can get a pissed off goddess off my tail."

"Anyone would want to get that addressed," Dart said.

All this attention was negatively affecting my actual goal, and Norma's.

We can use this to our advantage, she assured me.

"The snow is a lot of fun," Dart said loud enough for Silas to hear. "You should definitely build a snow ogre."

"Snow *man,*" Paolo corrected.

Dart shrugged. "You build your snow creature and I'll build mine."

I laughed and said, "I'll just help them build whatever they want, since it's their trip that I'm crashing."

"It's not crashing if you are invited," Dart countered.

I kicked a rock down the street. "I suppose, but it's their annual trip. I still feel like I'm imposing."

We made it out of the darker side of town and into the lively part where everyone knew Silas and Paolo.

Several women approached Silas at different times of our walk. He chatted cordially with them, but it was clear he was blowing them off.

"Why hasn't he ever been interested in other women?" I asked softly. "I've heard rumors even out in my small town that women have been throwing themselves at him and he's never seemed interested."

One of the girls who lived near me said she tried to convince him to go out to dinner with her and he politely, but firmly declined. She was the prettiest girl in our town, too.

"All I know is that when you went up on that stage, his entire demeanor changed," Paolo said. "I was already going to offer you a place, but when I saw his reaction, I was even more determined."

My ears burned and I turned so my hair covered my face.

Silas led us to a huge four-story building with flashing signs and a steady flow of customers in and out of the shop. "Ready to meet Martha?" He turned to face us and smiled as he asked, all signs of irritation gone. Was he just hiding it for now?

Paolo smoothed down his shirt and cleared his throat. "Do I look okay?"

"Very distinguished," Dart said, and I nodded in agreement.

Paolo inhaled and confidently walked up the steps and into the shop.

As soon as he stepped through the door, a huge red light shone onto Paolo, freezing him in place, and loud annoying alarms blared.

21

Dart and I covered our ears and cringed.

"How dare you!" a woman bellowed as she flowed down the stairs, customers parting for her in a hurry. Her power spun in a vortex around her, and I gaped at how powerful she was.

She was barely over five feet tall, fair-skinned, had the biggest set of boobs I'd ever seen, and curly brown hair that was almost a rat's nest in her vortex.

"Martha," he said, stepped out of the light, dropped to one knee, and took one of her hands to kiss the knuckles. "How is the most beautiful woman in the world?"

Immediately, all of her power disappeared, she snapped her fingers, and her appearance was fixed, her hair neatly brushed back into a ponytail, and the customers resumed their shopping like it was a normal occurrence.

"Annoyed you haven't visited in so long," she said and pouted down at him.

Dart and I looked at each other and then back at them.

Her attitude had changed so quickly that I felt nauseous.

Paolo stood and hugged her. "I'm sorry. The guild has me super busy. You know the guild drafts just happened."

She pouted more. "You still could have come to see me." She looked around him at us. "Oh, you two are new to his guild, right?"

We nodded and Dart stepped forward with a smile and a bow.

"I'm Dart, ma'am."

"Nadia," I said in introduction.

Silas stepped up behind me when a guy who was looking in a nearby display case got closer to me.

I huffed softly in annoyance, but knew he hadn't heard it.

"Come this way, children," she said and floated up the stairs before us.

Dart and I looked at Paolo, but he was already following her.

Obeying, we followed after them, maneuvering around all the other customers.

How could they stand to have so many people in one place? It was so crowded that it was almost impossible to see all the items available to buy.

Silas was behind me, but as we reached the next room, he laced our fingers together and immediately I felt a little less constricted.

Had he known?

She led us up another flight of stairs and to a room that was empty except for one woman behind the counter. The woman was tall, thin, and beautiful with dark red hair, a sleek pair of grey slacks and a button up white and black shirt. Her eyes sparkled when she saw Silas, but darkened when she saw our joined hands.

I gently pulled my hand free of his and looked at the closest display counter, trying to act like I hadn't seen her reaction.

"This is Priscilla," Martha introduced. "Priscilla, these are Dart and Nadia. They are new recruits to Golden Alicorn. I want you to gear them up while Paolo and I go talk."

I turned, mouth agape, thinking they were going to go make out or something, but both of them were frowning.

"Yes, ma'am," Priscilla said in a thickly accented voice.

"Behave," Paolo ordered us, but looked specifically at Dart.

Dart drew an X over his chest and smiled wide.

Once Paolo and Martha were gone, Priscilla looked at Silas and smiled. "It's been a few months, how are you, Silas?"

He leaned back against the display counter on his elbows and sighed. "A bit stressful, honestly."

She glanced at me. "Oh?"

"Nadia, look at this," Dart said, forcing me to look away from Silas and Priscilla, who started whispering to each other.

"Look at these daggers," he whispered and almost smooshed his face against the glass. "They've got the ability to automatically return to you after they're thrown."

"Sounds expensive," I whispered.

"Possibly," he agreed. "I wonder what kind of gear they're going to offer us."

"Only the finest," Priscilla said behind us.

I spun in surprise, fire in my hand.

She smiled. "Didn't mean to startle you."

I shook out my hand. "I'm so sorry."

"Silas tells me you prefer daggers and are fast. Did you see anything in the room you like?" she asked Dart.

"These daggers are awesome," he said and pointed in the case.

"Nadia," Silas called and waved me towards him on the opposite side of the room, where he was looking into a rack of weapons.

"Yeah?" I asked as I walked over.

"What do you think about using a rope dart as a weapon?" He pointed to a shiny silver one.

"Not really my style," I admitted and looked down at my hands. "Reminds me of my dad's whip too much."

"Ah, right. What about this?" He held out a metal rod about the size of a pen.

I took it and tilted it sideways. "What is it?"

Just as I asked, it made a weird sound and a metal shield wide enough to protect my torso was now in my hand.

"Whoa, that's cool," I whispered and made a flicking motion. The shield disappeared and became a rod again.

"I think you are severely lacking in the defense department," he said. "A shield or two would really benefit you."

"If it's something small like this that I can keep on me without lugging around a full shield, I am definitely open to it," I agreed.

"She should get some bracers!" Dart called out.

He wasn't wrong.

"Bracers would probably be a good idea," I said and chuckled. "But I don't have money for—"

"Don't worry about the money," Priscilla said. "This is covered by an agreement the two of them have had for over a decade."

Silas nodded. "I got geared up when I joined the guild, too."

"I don't really know what else I need or even want," I admitted. "I don't like to window shop because then I feel sad I can't get those things."

The fact that I had just said all that out loud shocked not just me, but Silas and Dart as well.

"Uh, sorry," I whispered, my face blazing hot.

"I've got you," Priscilla said. "I have a few items I think you'll find useful."

By the time she finished, I had new leather bracers, the shield Silas had shown me, and a secondary shield that only repelled magical attacks and not physical ones. It was a metal rod similar to the other, but the shield that came out was pure magic.

Luckily, my recent level up would allow me to use them at least a few times.

Paolo came out looking more worried than I had ever seen him, but he smiled when he saw our new items. "It looks like you have some excellent new items."

"Oh, and this," Priscilla said and tossed me a leather bag. "There are some snow clothes in there." She winked and I saw Silas scowl.

Had he told her?

"Th-Thanks," I whispered and put the bag on over my shoulder.

"Let's go. I'm sure the guild is being torn apart by some of our more rambunctious members," Paolo said.

We filed out of the shop and returned silently to the guild.

The four of us froze when we saw an all-out battle that spilled out of the main house and onto the front lawn.

"Aw, man! We missed the fun!" Dart whined.

Paolo smacked his staff into the ground and yelled, "Enough!"

Every single person froze, many with fists in mid-swing.

"Oh, hey!" Zachary called and finished his swing, punching a member whose name I didn't know in the stomach. He stood and dusted off his hands. "We were wondering when you might return."

"I'm far too sober for this," Paolo said and walked into the house.

"Was it something I said?" he asked, looking around.

Everyone got to their feet, dusted each other off, and walked inside like they hadn't just been beating the crap out of each other.

"Where were you guys?" Zachary asked. "I was hoping to convince Natalie to an arm-wrestling match."

"Nadia," Dart corrected.

"Get inside," Silas said and sighed. "You guys are always so much trouble. Can't you behave for one afternoon?"

Zachary slapped his hand against Silas's back and asked, "Where's the fun in that?"

A small girl on the porch caught my eye. "Who is that?" I asked Dart softly as we followed Zachary and Silas.

"Clair, she's an orphan that Zachary found on a

mission, and he brought her back here because she had nowhere else to go. The guild as a whole takes care of her."

"Lucky girl," I whispered.

She ducked her head when we approached.

Sometime, without her knowing, I'd give her a gift. Being an orphan wasn't easy, I'd seen several die in my hometown.

An explosion nearby made the ground quake and everyone stopped walking.

"Where did that come from?" Zachary asked, the normally easygoing guy suddenly very serious.

"The other house?" Silas said.

We all ran outside again and my mouth dropped when we saw what used to be one of the houses, just a smoldering pile of ash.

22

"Alarm!" Silas yelled.

Immediately, a shrill alarm began to blare.

"Where?" Dart asked, his daggers out and his back pressed to mine.

"I don't see anyone," I said.

It was the middle of the day, but there didn't appear to be any enemies that I could see.

Dart and I looked up at the same time, and had to dive away from each other as a meteor hit the spot we had just been.

In the sky, astride chimeras, were over a dozen people with white, expressionless masks on.

"White Chimeras!" Zachary yelled.

I picked myself up off the ground and ran towards the house porch where Clair cowered, her eyes wide as she stared up at them.

She screamed and I turned to see another meteor headed towards this house.

I stopped, spun around, and said, "Norma!"

All of my power, and some of Norma's, filled me. I used every ounce of the power, trying to deflect or at least redirect the meteor.

"Dart!" I screamed.

He ran past me, grabbed Clair from the porch, and ran in the opposite direction of the meteor.

The meteor slowed, but continued its progression towards the main house.

No! I couldn't let this happen. I couldn't let my new home be destroyed.

Zachary stepped next to me, glowed a bright purple, and began to push the meteor with his power as well. "Keep it steady, Nadia."

Pointing out that he remembered my name seemed trivial, so I just kept my power focused on the meteor that had stopped its approach and was beginning to move backwards.

"Plant your feet," he ordered. "I'm going to send it back. You might fall once it goes, so just release once you feel it go."

I nodded my understanding, too afraid to talk.

His eyes glowed purple, his body began to radiate power, and he screamed, "Suck it!"

The meteor streaked back towards the person who had sent it, hit the chimera they were riding, and knocked the rider to the ground.

Silas was immediately there, his sword through their chest. His black smoke spread around him like a cloak and I thought he had never looked so hot.

"Stop drooling," Dart teased as he ran by me.

The chimeras started swooping down, trying to use

their claws and stingers to attack our guild members.

Emily, a very low powered member, screamed and dove to the ground to avoid the claws, but the stinger swung towards her.

"Stop!" I yelled and released my wings to fly to her. I kicked the chimera in the side, and forced him away from her. I stood over her and exhaled. "You okay, Emily?"

"Yes," she sniffled. "Thank you."

"Can you get up?" I asked her.

"Not yet," she sniffled. "My legs are wobbly."

The chimera turned and roared at me.

"Bring it!" I shouted and pulled out my metal shield.

The chimera ran at me on the ground, its front claws digging into the dirt as it cantered towards me.

Using my wings to propel me forward, to keep it away from Emily, I slammed my shield into its face, and then lit the rider on fire.

The chimera spun in a circle, trying to dislodge the screaming and fire-covered rider.

Dart ran over, his daggers slicing faster than I could track, and killed both the rider and the chimera. He tipped an imaginary hat to me before running off to help others.

"He's so dreamy," Emily whispered on the ground behind me.

I looked at her and said, "You should tell him that."

Her cheeks turned bright red and she shook her head.

Clair screamed and all eyes turned to the chimera in the sky, the rider holding Clair by the back of her shirt.

Zachary froze in his battle against another chimera and it used the distraction to rake its claws across his chest. He grunted in pain, created a pillar of rock that sent the chimera flying away from him, and dropped to one knee.

"*Save her,*" Norma ordered me.

"You don't have to tell me," I snapped.

My rainbow hair glowed so brightly that the rainbow light bounced all around the ground and the building behind me. My black wings propelled me up into the air and straight at Clair.

I threw my sword and it stuck right into the rider's forearm. He screamed in pain and dropped Clair.

Flying faster, I caught her and tucked her against my chest as we made a circle back. "You okay?" I asked her.

She sniffled. "Thank you, Nadia."

I smiled. "Anytime."

Something struck one of my wings, piercing a hole through it.

I screamed in pain and started to fall out of the sky.

A fireball hit my other wing, burning a hole through it a well.

"Hold on!" I ordered Clair.

Retracting my wings fully so that they disappeared, I tucked Clair into my chest in as small of a ball as possible, and rolled on the ground to keep her safe as we hit.

The world went dark as pain exploded.

"Nadia!" Clair's voice called, but it sounded far away and her face swam in my vision like I was underwater.

Dart knelt by me and reached out towards me, but stopped. I saw his mouth moving, but couldn't hear him.

"No!" Silas yelled.

Black smoke exploded from him.

With the last bit of my strength and magical power, I

pulled out the magical shield I had and used it to protect Dart and Clair.

My eyes fluttered closed and I swam in the darkness, many voices including Norma's calling out to me, but none able to reach me in the dark depths.

Male voices yelled at me, but I couldn't see them.

I couldn't see anything.

What was this darkness? It wasn't Silas's, I knew what that was like.

Was this death's realm?

Or purgatory? Did purgatory even exist?

Had I been sent to another realm?

Try as I might to move or open my eyes, nothing worked.

Only darkness and numbness surrounded me.

A golden light shone in the darkness and three smaller golden lights shone off to the side of that one.

They blinked, like they were calling out to me.

The lights felt … familiar, but I didn't want to touch them. Something warned me not to touch them yet.

Pain filled me a moment, bright white light surrounded me, and then it was gone and the darkness returned.

The four lights moved closer together until they were right in front of me.

"No," I whispered in my mind. "Not yet."

The lights pressed forward, but I turned my back on them. No. I couldn't die yet.

That pain returned with the bright white light, and then I was lying on the ground of the front lawn with Tatiana, a healer, next to me.

"Did I die?" I asked as I gasped for air.

"Almost," she admitted and slumped to her butt on the ground.

Silas picked me up from the ground and hugged me tightly. "Fuck."

"I'm okay," I said, though his hug squeezed hard enough to hurt. "Is Clair—"

"I'm fine!" she chirped. "You saved me."

"Thank you," Zachary said.

Silas finally put me down and I faced him.

Zachary bowed at the waist. "I owe you a debt. Twice, you risked yourself. Thank you."

"No need to thank me. I would have done it for any member."

Paolo walked over and asked, "You okay?"

"Bruised, maybe broken, but I'll live." I gave him the best smile I could, considering I was hurting.

"You dropped this," Dart whispered and set the necklace the brothers had given me in my hand.

I tied it back around my neck. "Thank you."

"Status?" Silas asked.

"Three escaped," Zachary said and spit to the side.

"Who were they? I've never heard of that guild before."

Tatiana answered me. "They are a guild from across the ocean. We don't know why, but sometimes they come over and fight with guilds here. If they win, they boast about being stronger."

"Are we going to fight back?" Dart asked.

Zachary smacked a fist into his other palm and nodded.

"No," Paolo said. "We aren't going to leave the guild to fight them. We had some casualties, but nothing compared to them."

"Paolo," Silas snarled, "this is the second time they've attacked us. If we don't counter, they will view us as weak."

"I would rather they try to bring their entire guild here than we take ours to them. We should have the home advantage, not let them have it," Paolo said.

He was right, but it still left a bad taste in my mouth, and it seemed the others felt the same.

"I need a shower," I said and stretched slowly. Seemed like nothing was broken, which I counted as a win.

"Will your wings heal or are they permanently damaged?" Clair asked softly.

"They'll be healed by tomorrow," I assured her with a smile. "Come on, let's go use the baths."

"Can I come?" Emily asked.

I hadn't even noticed her. "Of course."

She pushed her glasses up her nose and smiled softly.

Once we were inside the house and made it to the women's bath, I asked, "What happened after I fell?"

Emily and Clair looked at each other before looking at me.

"A lot," Emily admitted.

"Let's wash and then while we soak in the hot water, you can fill me in, okay?"

They both agreed, and we stripped out of our dirty clothes, tossing them into the basket. The magic in the house would move them to the washing machines and by the time we finished, they would be on the table, washed, dried, and folded.

I helped Clair wash her hair and Emily helped wash mine. It was the first time I'd taken a bath like this in a few years, the last time having been with my sisters.

We all sighed as we slid into the hot water to soak once we were all fully cleaned.

"After you fell, Silas sort of exploded in black smoke," Emily said. "You pulled out a shield and the magic in it held the smoke back, protecting Dart, Clair, and I."

Clair nodded. "I thought it was going to smother us."

"Then, the chimeras started to try to flee," Emily continued. "Silas used the smoke, suffocating the chimeras and their riders. Some of them screamed while in the smoke. Some just disappeared. A few fell to the ground as …" She swallowed hard. "As skeletons."

"It was awesome," Clair said, her eyes wide as she recalled it. "We were all paying attention to him and didn't realize you had used your last bit of magic for the shield until it disappeared and your arms fell. Your heart stopped beating." She sniffled. "We thought you were dead."

"Dart started hitting your chest and Tatiana came over. When Silas finished killing all of the enemies that hadn't fled, he sucked all the smoke up and ran to you. He tried to give you some of his power, but it was like you were refusing it! He would push it towards you and then it would get shoved right back at him. Tatiana said she'd never seen that happen before." Emily took her glasses off to wipe the steam off. "Tatiana used some other power and it started your heart again."

"Did Silas hurt any of our people?" I asked softly.

Clair and Emily frowned as they thought about it and then both shook their heads.

I exhaled a huge breath of relief. "That's good."

"I think we would have been if you hadn't shielded us,

though. We were the closest to him," Emily said. She looked at me. "Are you two … together?"

"It's … complicated," I admitted and ducked my head under the water a second before I surfaced, spluttered, and wiped my face.

23

"It's obvious he cares about you," Clair said. "He doesn't react like that when others get hurt. I mean, he cares, but not so … emotionally."

"What do you guys do for fun?" I asked to change the topic.

"Oh, lots of things!" Clair said.

"We usually meet on Fridays to paint our nails," Emily said. "Would, would you want to join us?"

"I've never had my nails painted before," I admitted and looked at my torn up and chewed on nails.

Both of their mouths dropped.

"You definitely have to join us tomorrow!" Clair said. "I've got all the colors!"

"Black?" I asked, somewhat teasing.

She nodded. "*All* the colors."

"Sounds awesome. I would love to join you tomorrow."

She squealed and turned to Emily. "We should get out the jewels and try them again."

Emily nodded. "I bet I can get them to work this time."

Not sure what they were talking about, but not wanting to admit more of my ignorance, I just listened as they talked about jewels and glue.

We got out once our fingers were pruned and said bye as we went our different directions to our rooms.

I climbed the stairs in a trance, stopped only by Silas blocking my path.

"Can we talk?" he asked softly.

"Sure," I agreed with a nod.

He led the way to his room and I followed quietly, sitting on the edge of his bed as he closed the door behind him. He stared at the door a second before sitting beside me on the bed and flopping onto his back.

I stared at him lying on his back with his eyes closed for a second. "What's up?"

"I just … I just needed you to be next to me for a bit. So I could acknowledge that you are safe and alive," he admitted, eyes still closed.

"I heard you defeated most of the enemy forces with your smoke. So, now the entire guild knows. How are you feeling about that?"

He opened his eyes and turned his head so he could look at me. "I'd do it again in a heartbeat. They were aiming for you and if they hit you, you were going to die. You were already close to dying as it was. I couldn't let them kill you. I'd rather everyone in the world finds out what I am and what my powers are than let you get hurt." He sat up and glared at me. "Why did you reject my power?"

"What?" I asked. "When?"

"When you were dying, I tried to give you some of my power and you rejected it."

"I don't remember that at all. I was just swimming in darkness," I answered, but then recalled the golden lights.

Was that the guys trying to share their power with me, to keep me alive? If I had accepted it, what would have happened? Would I have sealed the bond like the lady had told us?

"Well, it worked out," I said and smiled wide. "We're both alive, the enemies are gone, and our guild is once again safe."

"Can you try to be a little less sacrificial?" he asked.

I glared at him. "Are you asking me to let a child get hurt? Not going to happen. I'd rather have my wings severed from my spine than let Clair fall to her death."

"I wasn't … I didn't …" he growled and sighed. "Just try to be a little bit more careful in the future, okay?"

"Well, I used the shields and they definitely helped," I said with a smile.

"Good," he said with a nod.

"So, you and Priscilla?" I asked, trying to look at him from the veil of my hair.

"What about us?" he asked.

"Were you two ever a thing?"

He smirked, leaned forward so he could see me beneath my hair, and asked, "Are you jealous, Nadia?"

I scoffed and flipped my hair over my shoulder. "No."

He smiled like I'd told him he had won a prize. "You are!"

On my feet, I headed towards the door. "I'm going to take a nap."

"Nadia's jealous," he sang.

I slammed his door shut to the sound of his laughter, but a smile split my face as I walked to my room.

24

"You're coming?" Grayson asked, eyes wide and sparkling with excitement.

I smiled and adjusted my bag. "I didn't bring the bag to tease you."

"Be careful with her," Silas said from the porch, "she's prone to sacrificial ideations."

I rolled my eyes and waved to Dart. "Keep an eye on him while I'm gone."

Dart leaned his elbow on Silas's shoulder. "We're going to spend the weekend too drunk to realize you're even gone."

"Cruel!" I teased, waved once more, and followed the trio off of Golden Alicorn grounds.

"So, did anything exciting happen while you were here?" Jasper asked, trying to sound nonchalant and completely failing.

I looked at them and sighed. "You guys know about the attack?"

"The entire city was gossiping about it," Parker

explained. "We almost came over here, but we knew if you needed us, you would have summoned us."

I flinched and looked at my feet as we walked. "Right."

"Nadia," Parker pushed.

I sighed. "I might have, a little bit, almost … died."

"I knew it!" Grayson yelled. "That's what that pain was."

"Why didn't you summon us?" Jasper asked calmly.

"It was a guild battle and I didn't really think about it, since I was too busy trying to protect some of my guild members."

"You didn't think about it?" Grayson gaped.

I shrugged. "Sorry."

"Sorry?" Parker groaned. "Dammit, Nadia."

"Wait, what did you mean about pain, Grayson?"

He looked away from me and whistled, the spitting image of his grandfather when he ignored me.

Walking through the town with this group was much different than when I had walked through here with my guild. Sure, some waved hello to the guys, but most just stared.

"Did you guys do something crazy on your recent mission?" I asked.

"Why would you ask that?" Parker asked.

"People are looking at you strangely," I commented.

"It's just our good looks that are distracting them," Jasper said with a smirk.

Although that was a possibility, it was not why so many people were looking at them.

"We might have had a little craziness on our mission," Grayson admitted.

"Such as?" I prompted.

Jasper sighed. "I destroyed the city hall for a small town." He quickly added, "On accident!"

"You go giant size and step on it?" I asked with a smirk.

He scowled. "Did someone already tell you?"

Laughter burst out of me. "No, I just guessed. I can't believe you stepped on a building!"

"Thankfully, no one was inside, but we had to give up our payment so they could rebuild," Parker said.

I shook my head and laughed as we finished our walk to the portal center. Shockingly, there were only a handful of people in line.

"Is that a shield?" Parker asked, his eyes down at my hip.

I grabbed the metal rod, flicked it to activate it, and held it out. "Pretty cool, right?"

Parker took it, flicked it, examined it, and activated it again. "This is cool."

"Check out this one," I said and showed him the magical one.

"Where did you get this?" Grayson asked and took the metal shield.

"Martha's," I answered.

"That place is always super crowded," Jasper commented with a scowl. "I hate going in there."

I nodded. "I started to get a little claustrophobic, but we went to a floor that was mostly vacated." I held up my arm, pulled back my jacket sleeve, and showed my bracers. "Got these, too."

"Nice," Jasper said. "I may have to force myself to go there soon."

"Dart got a dagger that can be called back to the owner," I added.

"Oh, I have that," Grayson said and pulled out his dagger. "Grandad made it for me."

It was still weird to hear someone refer to Loki as their grandad.

"That's awesome," I said. "I need to find a sword that does that."

"A sword that appears back in your sheath would be super handy," Jasper agreed with a nod.

"Next!" one of the workers called.

I put my stuff back away and followed them towards the portal.

Grayson went through first.

"You next," Jasper ordered me.

I nodded and stepped through.

Cold air blasted into my face and against my body, making me stumble a step sideways.

Grayson grabbed me and pulled me away from the portal and into his arms, cocooning me in his warmth. "You okay?"

"Just a bit shocking," I said with a smirk. "Didn't expect a strong wind when I stepped through."

"Good thing a strong guy was here to help you." He winked at me and it suddenly got warmer.

"Let's go," Jasper said.

Grayson pulled up the hood of my jacket and I was incredibly glad for the waterproof boots I had on, since we were standing in snow that went to the middle of my shin.

I stepped back from him and finally looked around. Beautiful white snow covered everything, the ground, the bushes, and the trees. About five hundred feet away I could see a frozen lake and a log cabin on the far bank with a fishing dock out into the water … ice. The cabin had snow on the roof, but a path was cleared to the front door.

"It's gorgeous," I whispered.

"Come on, let's get inside so you can put your bag away," Parker said.

As we walked, I moved slowly, one foot after the other, but the guys were just trudging forward and were quickly leaving me behind.

I tried to move faster, but kept sinking in the snow. "How are you walking so fast?" I called out.

Grayson turned and smirked. "It's a benefit of our genetics." He walked back, picked me up in a bridal carry, and walked the rest of the way to the cabin carrying me.

"You mean the snow doesn't hinder you?" I asked.

He nodded. "We're able to traverse it relatively easily. Most of the time, we won't sink in the snow even if people as light as you would."

"Damn lucky genetics," I muttered.

"I'm surprised you don't burn through the snow since you're so fiery," Grayson teased.

Parker opened the door and Grayson set me down on my feet inside the entryway.

The cabin already had a fire going in the fireplace, a couple of couches, a huge kitchen, and one entire wall that was just floor-to-ceiling glass so you could look out at the lake.

I walked towards the glass wall and stared. This was definitely a view I could get used to. A huge deer with the largest antlers I had ever seen walked across the ice with five small does behind him.

"That buck has been here for over a decade," Jasper said

softly beside me. "We watched him grow from a small fawn into that."

"Is he magical?" I asked.

"Nope," Jasper said. "Just magnificent."

"So, you guys won't kill him?" I guessed.

"Correct. He is going to live out his life until he dies of old age or some young buck kills him to take his herd."

"My bets on old age," Grayson said from the kitchen.

I turned and asked, "Why is your kitchen larger than the living room?"

"We spend most of our time in the kitchen," Grayson answered. "We're very food motivated."

"Noted."

He frowned and then laughed.

"Do you know how to cook any special dishes?" Grayson asked.

My cheeks warmed and I looked down. "I can cook stew." Admitting that the stew would contain pretty much whatever food we had on hand or could hunt would only embarrass me, so I kept that to myself.

"We love stew," Parker said.

"Would you cook it for us sometime this weekend?" Jasper requested. "We can hunt whatever meat you need."

"The recipe takes whatever meat you have on hand," I explained. "And basic spices that most houses have in the cupboards."

"Will you cook it tomorrow night?" Parker asked.

I looked up. "You guys really want me to cook for you?" They all nodded.

"It might not be very good," I admitted. We were always

starving when we ate it and even food we normally hated tasted good.

"Please?" Grayson urged.

I couldn't say no to that. "Okay, but don't be upset if it doesn't taste good."

"Let me show you your room," Parker said and headed down the hallway.

I followed behind him, feeling a little more nervous about the weekend and my plans.

He stopped at the first door and pushed it open. "This will be your room." He pointed at the door across from it. "Mine." He pointed at the other two. "Grayson and Jasper."

"Okay," I said and stepped inside the room they had assigned me. It was larger than the one I had back at the guild and had a bed with silk netting, a dresser, wash basin, high-backed chair, and a loveseat that looked out the window over the lake.

"Whoa," I whispered as I walked over to the window and sat on the edge of the loveseat.

"We thought you would appreciate the view more than us. We're a little spoiled, I suppose since we've seen it so many times."

"I could live here and stare at this view forever," I said softly.

"Are you agreeing to live with us, Nadia?" he asked in my ear.

25

I yelped and stood. "N-No. I-I-I…"

He winked at me. "Just teasing you. Why don't you get settled and then get dressed to go play in the snow?"

"Play?" I asked.

"We'll take you sledding before it gets too dark," he said with a nod. He shut the door behind him, leaving me no chance to ask any other questions.

Instead of staring out the window like I wanted to, I changed into more suitable clothes, including a fur-lined beanie and waterproof gloves. I also added a little bit of eye makeup that Emily had given me and insisted I put on when I arrived.

"If you're wrong, Emily, I get to paint your face like a clown," I whispered to myself to try to imbue a bit of courage.

The guys were waiting on the front porch and turned when I came out. All three stared at me, silent, for a long time.

"What's wrong?" I asked.

"We were just inspecting you to make sure you were ready for the snow," Grayson said, but it felt like a lie.

"Ready?" I asked.

"I'm going to carry you again," Grayson said and cleared his throat. "To make the trip to the hill faster."

I sighed softly, but nodded. "Okay." Holding them up would be more embarrassing than having him carry me.

Grayson reached towards me, but Jasper picked me up instead. "My turn to carry her," he said.

"Okay," Grayson agreed and started heading towards the trees.

Parker waited for Jasper to go next and walked behind us, carrying a large wooden sled.

"Do the wild animals attack you?" I asked. There had to be large predators out here.

"We haven't had too many issues with them, but you shouldn't wander off on your own," Jasper said.

"That was not why I was asking," I said with a chuckle. "I'd probably get lost and freeze to death on my own."

"Are you wearing the necklace?" he asked.

I nodded and patted my upper chest. "Beneath my layers."

"Good," he said with a nod and his hold on me tightened slightly.

"How's it going with your guild?" I asked. "You guys haven't told me much about it or how you're fitting in."

"Things are going well," Parker answered behind us.

I turned and leaned my chin on Jasper's shoulder so I could look at him. "Yeah?"

He nodded. "Being demigods makes it a little easier to join most institutions. Plus, our powers are very useful on missions, and we go on missions more often than most of their older members. We've brought a lot of good publicity to the guild and decent commissions."

A smile split my face as I pictured the three working together and then returning to the guild with a sack of money for the guild's commission.

"What about the other members?"

"There were a few who challenged us in the first week, but things have quieted down," Grayson answered.

I turned around to look at him, but he wasn't facing us. "That's pretty standard from what I hear." Thankfully, aside from the jerk recruit in the very beginning, I hadn't had any issues.

"The worst part is the women," Jasper grumbled.

My eyes snapped up to his. "What?"

"They keep throwing themselves at us, sneaking into our room so they're in one of our beds when we return, and other ridiculous things. The guild master had to make an announcement that they were all to stop such foolishness, and it earned us some ridicule from the males who desire that type of attention." He scowled as he answered, seeming honest.

"You … don't want women to want you?"

All three stopped walking at the same time and moved into a standing pattern that allowed me to see them all without turning my head. It was something they did often, but I hadn't noticed it until now.

"We only want you," Grayson said.

"That type of attention is not what we want," Jasper added.

"The only woman we want to sneak into our rooms or throw themselves at us, is you," Parker agreed.

My cheeks warmed and I had to resist the urge to fan my face. "You're such flatterers."

"We're serious," all three said simultaneously.

I smiled so wide I worried my face might split. "Well, that's good to know."

This was the perfect time to ask them about the test, but we hadn't spent enough time together yet. I didn't want to ruin the rest of our time here if the conversation didn't finish favorably.

They resumed walking, saving me from figuring out my dilemma.

We finally made it to the top of the hill, and Parker set the sled down.

Jasper set me on the front of the sled, sat behind me, and said, "Hang on!"

Before I could ask anything, he pushed us forward and we slid down the hill we'd just climbed up. I had seen people sledding before, but never realized how fast you went.

I squealed in joy as we flew down the hill and momentarily went airborne after hitting a rock.

Jasper leaned to the right, making us turn and head towards the side of the hill we'd climbed up.

The sled stopped and I jumped up, eyes wide and a huge smile splitting my face. "Again!"

Jasper chuckled and asked, "You enjoyed that?"

I nodded emphatically. "I never realized how fun that was!"

"Well, let's hurry to the top and do it again, then," Jasper said, grabbed the sled in one hand, and picked me up under his arm, carrying me sideways like one might a toddler.

He ran up the hill really fast and stole my breath. Were they holding back most of the time for me?

"My turn!" Parker said and took the sled from Jasper.

I sat on the front and he pulled me back to sit closer to him, his legs on either side of me.

"Ready?" he asked.

I nodded. "Yes."

He pushed off and I squealed in joy again as we zoomed down the hill.

Up, down, up, down, and repeated until the sun set and the boys said it was too dark to continue sledding safely.

My cheeks hurt from smiling so much. I rode piggyback on Parker instead of having him carry me in his arms, which he seemed fine with. "So, what are we doing tomorrow?" I asked and rested my chin on his shoulder so I could look at his face while I spoke.

"We're going to build a snowman," he answered and turned his head to look at me. "Or whatever creature you want to try to build."

"Sounds fun," I replied. "Though, I don't know if anything will be as fun as sledding was."

"Uh oh, guys, I think we set the bar too high," Parker teased his brothers.

They chuckled, but didn't reply.

"We should get changed and use the magic water pool," Grayson suggested.

"Magic what?" I asked, thoroughly intrigued.

"It's a stone circle with water in it, and when you put some of your magic into the crystals inside it, the water warms and bubbles like a hot spring. It's seriously one of my favorite things about this cabin," Grayson answered.

"I'm totally in for that!" I said, but then quickly added, "I don't have a bathing suit, though."

"Shirt and shorts or something works," Parker said.

"We have something you can borrow if you need to," Grayson offered. "I'm pretty sure Parker's shirt would be long enough on its own for you to wear."

"Okay," I agreed.

After changing into one of Parker's shirts that went all the way to mid-thigh, I followed the guys out a back door and immediately shivered in the cold, glad I had on shoes so I wasn't walking in the snow that covered the back porch.

"Don't worry, you'll get warmed up in just a second," Jasper promised.

They put the towels we'd brought into a little wooden cabinet on the edge of the porch to keep them safe from the snow. We also put our shoes inside before quickly climbing into the circular stone pool of water.

It was lukewarm, which surprised me, since they hadn't used magic yet.

"There are grooves you can sit in, carved into the stone," Parker said. "Pick your spot."

Since it was circular, there didn't really seem to be a better spot. I chose one that let me look out over the frozen lake and at the woods instead of at the house, though.

Once I sat, the guys played several games of ro-sham-bo before taking seats around me, Parker on my right, Jasper on my left, and Grayson facing me.

"Ready?" Grayson asked.

I nodded.

Parker closed his eyes, power grew around him, and after several silent moments, small crystals embedded in the pool started to glow a bright blue as he put his power into them.

The water warmed, started to bubble, and bubbled higher.

I worried it was going to bubble too much, but it maintained its level and I sighed as the water warmed so much that the cold wind outside didn't bother me.

"Okay, this is amazing," I said. "If I ever own a place, I'm definitely getting one of these installed."

"Where would you own land?" Jasper asked.

Pausing, I scowled. "Um, well, since I never really thought it was possible, I hadn't thought about it."

"Would you rather be near a beach, in the forest, or in the city?" Grayson asked.

"I like being in the city, because then you are close to a lot of stores and activities," I admitted. "But having a place out in the forest where no one could find you or bother you would be nice, too. That's more of a retirement idea, I guess, than anything, and I'd be worried about forest fires possibly destroying the house. The beach might be nice, but I've heard about the crazy storms that happen on the beach and wouldn't want my house destroyed from one of those."

"You could put protections up so the storms didn't destroy your house," Jasper said.

"Those aren't one hundred percent effective," I said.

"You're not a very cup half full person," Jasper teased.

"I prefer to be prepared for the worst possible scenario,

which normally occurs in my experience." Or perhaps that was just my curse.

"*You are pretty cursed,*" Norma commented.

She wasn't wrong.

"What about a snowy place like this?" Parker asked. "There's not crazy weather that happens here and, in the summer, the ice melts and the area is gorgeous and the lake is full of fish to eat."

"That sounds nice," I admitted and sighed. "But that's all a long way off, if ever. What about you guys? Where do you all want to live?"

"We've talked about Jotunheim," Grayson said. "Grandma has some land she would sell us."

"Grandpa also has some land he said he's holding until we find our mate. He won't tell us where it is, though," Parker added.

Their mate. The thought that it might not be me hurt more than I wanted to admit. I was pretty sure they were my soulmates, but if they weren't, letting them go would be really painful.

Maybe I shouldn't get closer to them this weekend?

Grayson leaned across the pool and kissed me on the lips.

I blinked a few times as he sat back, smiling. "What was that for?"

"You looked sad and I thought a kiss might get rid of the frown. It worked." He winked.

I shook my head and laughed. These guys were something else.

"I definitely didn't hate it," I admitted.

Jasper turned my head to the side to look at him and kissed me, slowly at first, deepening it as we continued.

Parker set his hand on my knee and rubbed it up and down.

I turned to look at him and he kissed my cheek and down my neck.

I gasped softly as he nipped at my neck and Grayson knelt in front of me, licking his lips.

"Are you really going to give me that baby already?" Norma asked.

Her voice jolted me out of my lustful haze and I jerked back from the guys. "Um, I, uh …"

She totally just killed the whole vibe.

"I'm sorry, the demon is talking and ruining things," I admitted. It was probably better to be honest than make them think something was wrong with them or I didn't want to continue.

"It's okay," Grayson said as he sat back in his spot. "It would be weird to have someone else in my head when I'm trying to be intimate with another person."

"Sorry," I said, feeling like I had ruined things.

"Well, this just gives us more time to get to know you and ask you things," Jasper said, smiling sweetly.

These guys really were great.

And Norma was an asshole.

26

The last day of our trip arrived and I gnawed on the inside of my cheek in worry.

How would they react? Would they agree or get mad?

"What's on your mind?" Grayson asked and traced the tip of his finger down between my eyebrows to the tip of my nose.

"I have something to discuss with you all and I'm worried how you'll react and answer," I admitted. "I've been waiting because I didn't want to ruin our trip, but I need to discuss it before we get back and go to our separate guilds."

"Best to just rip the hangnail off now before it becomes infected," Norma agreed.

Folding my legs beneath me on the couch, I stared at the trio, who took seats on the couch opposite me. Hopefully, this went well.

"Please, go ahead," Jasper said, ever the respectful one.

After a deep breath, I just blurted it out. "I think you three are my soulmates, but I think that Silas might be one as well. He kissed me, by the way. I went to meet a woman who had multiple soulmates and she told my guild master about a test we could do to confirm we were soulmates or not, but there is a potential side effect he wasn't too happy about. The decision is completely up to you three, and I know we haven't been dating that long, and I know that you said you didn't want me to believe Voluptua and wanted to build our relationship naturally, but—"

"We'll do it," Grayson answered.

"We are willing to do anything if it will put your mind at ease," Jasper said.

Parker nodded his agreement as well.

I stared at them in silent disbelief for a long moment, shocked because I honestly hadn't expected them to answer so quickly.

My upper body sagged in relief. "Thank you."

"If we are your soulmates, are you willing to leave your guild and join ours?" Grayson asked. "I don't like the thought of you almost dying while we aren't there to help you."

"I can't leave my guild," I said. "Silas is there, and—"

"Silas is supposed to be one of the most powerful men in history, but you almost died on his watch. That doesn't make us feel better to know he's there," Parker said, his voice clipped and words stern.

"It wasn't his fault," I countered, but stopped my argument and sighed. "While I would prefer to be in the same guild as you, I don't want to leave mine. I'm sorry."

All three scowled and looked at each other.

"We'll discuss it more after we confirm we are your soulmates," Jasper said.

Confirm. They already believed they were. Honestly, so did I, but I still felt it was a good idea to get the official confirmation. If only it were simpler to know who your soulmate was. It didn't make any sense to me that we could have soulmates and never truly know who they were.

"I thought you said you didn't believe in it and not to think too hard about it?" I reminded them.

"We wanted to get to know you better and try to confirm more ourselves," Jasper said.

"You're scowling," Grayson commented.

A laugh escaped me. "So are the three of you."

They all laughed as well.

Looking out the window, I swore I saw a dark shadow dash across the field. Was I hallucinating?

"I saw it, too," Norma said and I heard fear in her voice. *"There's a demon nearby."*

"There's a demon nearby," I relayed as I stood and let some of my power out, my hair casting rainbows on the walls.

"How do you know?" Grayson asked, looking out the window.

"Norma feels it," I answered truthfully. "Is it him?" I asked her.

"I can't be sure. We leveled up, but it's too soon for him to have pinpointed us. I thought we would have more time."

"Should we run or face it?" I asked Norma and out loud.

"Run," Norma said.

"Face it," Grayson said.

"Run," Jasper and Parker said.

"Three votes for run," I advised them. "Two votes to

face it. Sorry, Grayson, it looks like you and I were outvoted this time."

"Grab your things and let's go," Jasper ordered and dashed to his room.

Grumbling my irritation, I went to my room and threw all my stuff back into my backpack, put my snow clothes on, secured my backpack, and drew my sword. Even if we were running, that didn't guarantee the demon wouldn't come after us, and I didn't want to be unarmed.

When I made it to the front door, the trio were already there, waiting, with weapons drawn and their power swirling around them in preparation of being used.

"If we end up needing to flee, we're going to pick you up, okay?" Grayson advised.

I nodded, despite how much I wanted to argue. It was smarter to allow them to carry me than to slow them down and risk getting them hurt or killed. "I can fly," I advised them.

The three turned and blinked at me.

"What?" Jasper asked.

"When Norma allows me more of my power and a little of hers, I have wings." They were technically *her* wings, but I didn't want to go into that.

"That would have been incredibly useful to know before," Parker grumbled.

"Let's go," Grayson said. "I can feel that darkness getting closer."

With our weapons at the ready, we walked out into the snow and headed towards the portal to return.

"I'm going to give you more than usual," Norma warned me. *"The demon is really close."*

Before I could respond, she opened up the container and I gasped and moaned as my magic filled me. So much.

"Whoa," Grayson breathed and stopped to stare at me. He stepped forward, put his hand on my cheek, and kissed me deeply.

"Focus," Jasper growled.

Grayson pulled back from me and opened his mouth.

Whatever he was about to say was cut off when a dark blur streaked towards us.

I shoved Grayson to the side and swung my sword in an upwards curve.

The demon leaned to the side, avoided my blade, and grabbed me by the throat.

"It's him!" Norma screamed in my mind.

"I've been looking for you, Traitor," the demon growled in my face. He was tall, wide, and powerful … so powerful. He made me want to cower in a way that not even the gods did.

Jasper swung his sword at the demon at the same time that Parker lashed out with his magic.

The demon flew up into the air, carrying me by the throat with him. "You're coming with me to answer my questions," he growled.

"No," I hissed and covered him in fire.

The demon smiled.

The bastard smiled!

"Thanks, it was getting chilly in this snow," he taunted.

Norma released most of my power and a tad of hers. *"Kill him!"*

Without air to my lungs and brain, I was going to black out, or die soon.

I stabbed the demon with my sword through his stomach, punched him in the face, lit him on fire again, and poured all of my magic into each attack.

The demon grunted, narrowed his eyes in annoyance, and touched my forehead. "Sleep."

"Nadia!" Parker yelled.

"We can't shoot at him from this far away or we might hit her," Grayson growled.

The trio shifted into their larger forms, making the demon hesitate, but only for a second.

For whatever reason, his sleep spell just made me groggy instead of putting me fully to sleep. I felt like I'd only had two hours of sleep and needed a gallon of coffee.

"You've made some interesting friends," he commented. "Sadly, it's not enough." He snapped his fingers and the trio collapsed on the snow; their bodies reverted back to their normal sizes.

Fury, worry, and panic filled me. A high-pitched ringing grew louder and louder in my ears as I stared at the trio, who I was fairly certain I was falling in love with.

My mind went blank, not even Norma's voice reached me, though I could sense her trying to speak.

Grabbing the demon's wrist that held my throat, I released my wings, flapped to level myself, and twisted the wrist.

The demon's bone shattered, he screamed, and his hand dropped limply. I was freed.

Instead of putting distance between us, I yanked my sword from his stomach, swung it in an upwards arc, sliced through his stomach and chest, and cut into his chin.

He fell backwards, crying out in pain from the deep

cuts and landed on the ground, the snow around him turning red from his blood.

I flapped my wings once and then folded them in as I dove towards him, like an eagle diving for a fish in the water.

He drew a strange black weapon that reeked of evil.

As I drew near, I made my wings disappear, spun to the left, and as my body rotated, I sliced into him with my sword and activated my shield, so his weapon couldn't touch me.

His swing was strong, despite him being so injured, and it knocked me ten feet away.

I landed and rolled in the snow before hopping to my feet and clanging my sword against my shield. "Come at me!"

The trio lay near him and I needed to draw him away, to protect them.

The demon growled. "Face me yourself, you coward. Stop hiding within that human's body."

He was talking to Norma.

"She doesn't need to waste the magic to come face you here, when I can kill you and I'm weaker than her," I taunted.

"She knows I will find her and destroy her," he spat. "She must die for being a traitor!"

"I'm no traitor!" Norma roared from my mouth, our voices a combined and terrible sound. "I am the one who was betrayed! He was my mate and she stole him, against his will. Her death was too quick. I should have made the bitch suffer."

The demon bellowed. "She was your queen! She was your sister!"

"She stopped being my sister the moment she laid her filthy claws on my mate!" Norma snapped.

My heart hurt for Norma and I felt tears in my eyes.

"If she were a good queen, she wouldn't have sent you to kill me," Norma said. "You should have denied her dying request and let me live out the rest of my life in my home."

"Let's end this," I whispered to Norma. "Let's make him pay for chasing you from your home."

With most of my powers at my disposal, and Norma lending me some of hers, I knew I could do this. I could defeat him.

The demon snarled and then swung his sword at Grayson's unconscious form.

I screamed and raced forward, but I wouldn't make it.

With a silent prayer to every god in existence, I threw my shield as I ran. The shield spun through the air and landed right over Grayson's chest as the demon's weapon lowered, and blocked it.

Disbelief widened the demon's eyes and gave me the distraction I needed to tackle him away from the guys.

As fast as I could, I pummeled his face with my fists, adding the rainbows my hair cast around my knuckles. The rainbow light created burns with each punch, and the demon cried out in pain and tried to knock me away from him.

I was unsure why or how I had thought of that, but ultimately happy it had worked.

The demon managed to knock me away, his blood staining the ground and my fists. "How could you have possibly become this strong in such a short time?" he panted.

Instead of answering, I grabbed him by the throat and stabbed him through the heart with my dagger.

"Go and be with your queen," Norma said through my voice.

The demon's mouth gaped open and he exploded into ash.

"It's sad that one little demon gave you so much trouble," a feminine voice said behind me. "At least it gives me the ability to do this." A clawed hand wrapped around my throat and a portal opened behind her.

27

"Nadia!" Grayson called out weakly as the three of them began to stir.

"Gray," I called out and reached for him. The way the demoness held me prevented me from seeing what she looked like, or even moving beyond lifting my hand. She was *so* powerful.

The female demon chuckled and waved at the guys. "I'll send back the body so you can bury it."

Jasper ran towards us, but the demoness stepped through the portal, carrying me by my throat, and closed it just before Jasper could reach it.

The heat of hell pressed upon me, such a stark contrast to the snow we'd just been in that I panted.

Cold iron chains were secured around my wrists and ankles, and there was nothing I could do. I couldn't move.

"Rest. Tomorrow I'm going to pull that traitorous bitch out of you, so I can torture her. If you survive, I'll send you back to your home," the demoness said.

I looked up and my mouth dropped. She was beyond

gorgeous. Her appearance reminded me of a celestial being instead of a demonic one, though she did have horns atop her head. "Who are you?" I asked.

"*My sister,*" Norma whispered mentally.

"I am Queen of Hell," she answered with a sweet smile that showed off her wickedly sharp fangs. "Don't try to flee, or I'll rescind my agreement to send you home."

"My guild and my men will come looking for me," I warned her. "Just release me now."

"Oh, I do hope they come. I want to see these men. They looked powerful and I need more powerful males in my harem."

"You wouldn't," I gasped. "You wouldn't do the same as your other sister."

Her brow furrowed. "Is that what Normatoxaly thinks happened? No, child, that's not what happened. Tomorrow, I will explain everything."

With nothing left to do but relax and recuperate my strength to try to fight against the demoness tomorrow, I lay on my back and sighed.

"Are you alright?" I asked Norma. "I can't feel my magic or yours."

"*She sealed our magic via these magically enchanted irons,*" she explained.

"Wonderful," I grumbled and sighed.

Despite it being hot, and knowing I should probably be uncomfortable; I enjoyed the heat and wasn't even sweating. It felt relaxing, which was definitely strange.

Would anyone be able to find me? Were we in some version of the Underworld or some alternate dimension? I wasn't even sure anymore. What were the rules governing the gods and their ability to travel between them?

Were Thor or Loki able to travel here, or were they only allowed to travel to their places? If not, did that limit the brother trio since they were demigods?

"Our bargain has been fulfilled," I whispered to Norma. "We could separate now and you could be free, escape her imprisonment by not being here."

She was silent for so long that I thought our connection was blocked.

"*I don't want to end our partnership,*" she finally whispered.

"We've accomplished your goal," I reminded her. I had fulfilled the additional term to our contract, to destroy the one after her, the term I hadn't mentioned to anyone else for fear of their reaction.

She was silent and this time remained silent.

Time passed, I slept, and woke to the cell door being opened.

A male demon stood before me, his horns curved back over his head like slicked-back hair. "Follow me."

I stood and looked down at the chains. "I can't leave the room."

He rolled his eyes, flicked his finger at me, and the chains came unattached from the wall, but remained on my wrists and ankles, dragging behind me.

"Lead the way," I said and followed behind him out of the cell, down seven hallways, and finally to a large room made of black stones with strange symbols etched into them.

The demoness from the previous day sat on a throne on

the far side, a glass of dark red liquid in one hand. She smiled when I entered. "Welcome, child. Today, I will cure your demon problem."

"You said you would explain what had happened," I reminded her. "Will you tell me the full, true story before you remove the demon from me? Also, if you remove her, will that break the seal she has on the container that holds my magic?"

Her brows shot into her hairline. "She put your magic in a container?"

I nodded.

"That complicates things," she whispered and tapped a claw on the arm of her throne. "First, I will tell you what happened, as that will give me time to think as well."

The room was empty aside from her throne and a stone table. So, I hopped onto the stone table, arranged the chains in a more comfortable position, and crossed my legs.

Her lips twitched, amused by my antics, no doubt. "Normatoxaly was in love with a very powerful demon, we'll call him Dave. Dave loved her, but he also craved more power. He came to my sister, the then queen, and asked for her to accept him into her harem. In order to do that, she had to break his bond with Normatoxaly. He agreed."

"He wouldn't!" Norma bellowed from my mouth.

"He did," she growled. "He agreed to the breaking of the bond and the forming of the new one. However, there is always a risk when one bond breaks that it could kill one or both parties. He … did not make it."

I could feel Norma's sadness like it was my own. Tears

streamed down my face and dripped from my chin to my legs as pressure and pain built in my chest.

"I warned her against accepting him. I told her that you would never forgive her, but she was too greedy. You two always fought over the same toys and weapons. It shouldn't have surprised me when you fought over the same male as well." The demoness sighed and shook her head. "For what it's worth, I would have refused him." She stood and walked to me, grabbed the chains, and secured them on the side of the table in a metal binding. "Now, let's do this. Normatoxaly, release the girl's powers, break the container."

"No," Norma said from my throat.

"We have a contract," I reminded Norma, but said it out loud so her sister could hear.

"Give me one more week and I'll show you who your true soulmates are without you needing to do the spell," she offered.

"If you could show me who my true soulmates were, you would have offered sooner," I challenged.

"You have soulmates?" her sister asked. "As in … multiple?"

I nodded.

"How many?" she breathed and her power gathered around her like she felt threatened.

"Four," a familiar deep male voice said behind me.

"Silas!" I gasped and turned to look at him.

The demoness grabbed me by the throat and stood so her body was hidden behind mine. "No!" she growled.

Silas looked me over and smiled. "Have a good trip?"

"It was nice," I said. "Cold, but nice."

The black smoke swirled around him and his eyes glowed red. "Don't worry, I'm here to take you home."

"Why are you here, Silas?" the demoness asked and her chest rumbled with a growl.

"She's my soulmate," he answered. "And you kidnapped her."

"No," she exhaled softly.

"You stole her from three demigods," he told her. "They're wreaking havoc in your courtyard right now."

"Who are you?" she asked me as she stepped to the side to look at my face.

"She's mine," Silas said. "Let her go and I'll let you live, Vonnamik."

Vonnamik growled. "My sister is inside her. I brought her here to remove her."

That made Silas pause. He tilted his head to the side. "You can remove her?"

Vonnamik nodded. "She already fulfilled the contract, anyway. I heard her say it."

Silas looked at me. "You fulfilled it? How? It hasn't been the time or …" His eyes dropped to my stomach.

"There was a third clause," I said quickly so he wouldn't get the wrong idea. "I killed the demon who had been after her."

His shoulders sagged in relief. "Demoness, break the container and release her."

"Norma," I whispered.

"She's going to kill me," Norma whispered, sounding afraid.

"You're stronger now," I reminded her. "It's time for you to face your fears."

Just like it was time for me to face mine.

"Release the chains so I may break the container," Norma said from my mouth.

I really hated that.

"One iron," Vonnamik countered and unlocked my right wrist.

There was silence as Vonnamik, Silas, and I stared at each other, and I held still despite wanting to fidget or ask questions.

The sounds of fighting grew louder the longer we waited.

A huge crash sounded, shaking the building so much I fell off the table and to the ground.

The container that my magic had been sealed in exploded and it all returned to me. It was like a tidal wave of power, almost too much for me to accept.

My body arched up and I moaned. My rainbow hair glowed and lit up the dark room brighter than noon on a cloudless day.

"What is she?" Vonnamik asked and stepped back from me.

"Perfect," Silas answered and walked towards me. "Nadia?"

The power on top of Norma being inside of me was too much. I felt like I was going to explode.

I was too full. There was too much! Too much!

"Get her out," I begged. "Get her out!"

His smoke covered the chains and the chains instantly disappeared. More power poured into me and I threw my head back as I screamed.

"I was trying to protect you," Norma admitted. *"You're far*

more powerful than you realize. I'm sorry. I'm so sorry I was so weak."

Vonnamik grabbed my head and chanted in the demonic tongue.

"Live your life," I whispered mentally to Norma. *"You're stronger than you realize. You can be queen if you want. Do what you want with your life. You don't need me. You can accomplish what you want now without my involvement."*

The bond between Norma and I stretched, making my body arch up, and as it snapped, I screamed.

It felt like an organ had been pulled from my body and blood was pouring out.

"Help her!" Silas ordered.

Norma materialized beside me, more beautiful than the queen with large horns, and squatted down. "Shit. I hadn't realized our bond was so tight."

"She's going to die," Vonnamik whispered. "It's like when a mate bond is severed. She can't survive that."

The door exploded as Jasper, Grayson, and Parker stormed inside, eyes glowing.

"Where is she?" Grayson demanded.

Vonnamik pointed at me on the floor.

"What do we do?" Silas asked them.

Clutching at my chest, I tried to put pressure, like one would on a physical wound, but it did nothing. "It hurts!" I cried. "It hurts so much."

"I'm sorry," Norma whispered as she backed away from me, clutching her own chest. "I'm so sorry, Nadia."

"Her bond was severed and now she's hemorrhaging," Vonnamik explained to the trio.

"We have to make our bonds with her," Jasper said.

"No," Silas growled.

"All of us," Jasper added. "We can see it. We saw it the day she almost died. All four of us."

"What if you're wrong?" Grayson whispered and dropped to his knees beside me. "What if we're wrong?"

"I'll die before I let her die," Parker said and dropped to his knees as well.

"You'll die if you're wrong," Silas said.

Rolling onto my side, I coughed up blood and gasped for air as the pressure built in my chest. Black spots formed around the edges of my vision.

"Norma," I cried and reached out towards her.

"I'm sorry," she sobbed, tears in her red eyes, and ran from the room.

"Let's do this," Silas said and dropped to his knees at my head.

Silas placed a hand on my upper right shoulder. Jasper placed a hand on my left arm. Grayson placed a hand on my left thigh. Parker placed a hand on my right thigh.

All four closed their eyes and drew on their powers.

Still gasping in pain, I watched as four golden ropes slid out of my chest and towards each of the guys.

Oh, shit. I did have soulmates … four of them.

The ropes connected to their chests and golden light exploded out from us.

My ears rang and my vision spun.

"Nadia," Silas whispered.

The pain was gone and I felt whole again.

"You came for me," I whispered. "You four came for me."

"Of course we did," Grayson said, threading our fingers together.

"We're sorry we couldn't protect you," Jasper said and squeezed my leg.

"We tried to get to you, but we couldn't find the correct path," Parker said.

"Even grandpa was pissed that he couldn't find the way to you," Grayson added.

"How did you find me then?" I asked and blinked away the dark spots so I could see them clearly.

"This is my home realm," Silas answered. "If I had known that your demon was from here, I could have forced her out of you easily, but you kept her name a mystery."

"Is she …"

"She's gone," he answered and stroked my cheek. "She fled."

28

With her gone, out of my head, I didn't really know how to feel or act. I had been merged with her for so long that it just felt … weird.

I felt … naked. Like a part of me was missing. Would this heal? Would I feel better after some time?

"What now?" I asked and shoved the worries about Norma down.

"Now, we take you home so you can recuperate," Silas answered and stood.

"How is this going to work?" I asked as I sat up and looked at the trio. "You aren't part of our guild and I don't want to leave this guild."

"Actually, we were planning to petition Marco to allow us to join your guild," Jasper admitted. "We didn't want to say anything to you just in case it was denied."

I looked at Silas.

He smiled and said, "They won't be denied now."

"What about your guild?" I asked. "You chose them and—"

"We choose you," Grayson said and squeezed our still interlocked fingers. "You're what's important to us, not the guild."

"Your mom—"

"Is an old fool," Hel said as she walked into the room.

"What are you doing here?" Silas asked and stepped between us.

She raised both hands. "I come in peace and received approval from your father."

Silas relaxed at that, but it made me curious who his father was.

Hel stepped around him and glared down at me. "I still don't like you, but I saw you protect my sons and saw the love you feel for them. Plus, I can see your soul bonds. I won't get between soulmates, even if it pisses me off."

"Mom," Jasper sighed.

"What I'm trying to say is," Hel said with a deep scowl. "Thank you for protecting my sons and … welcome to the family."

The last part was whispered, but I still heard it.

Jasper helped me stand and hugged me tightly. "We were so scared."

"Where's the queen?" I asked and looked around.

"She went after Norma," Silas answered.

"Wait, you said you're from here?" I asked.

He nodded. "My father is a god here."

"Is … is he the one I spoke to?"

Silas's eyes widened. "What? You spoke to him?"

"Does your smoke not hurt me because we're soulmates?" I asked. That would make sense, but it could be other reasons, too.

"I'm not sure." He looked down at his feet with a scowl.

"Can we leave?" Grayson asked. "It's really hot here."

"Is it? I'm actually really comfortable," I admitted.

Silas lifted his head and smiled. "Would you like a tour before we leave?"

"Excuse me," Hel said, reminding me that she was still there.

"Sorry," I apologized and bowed. "Thank you for coming ... and apologizing."

"Boys, come see me in two days," she ordered.

"Okay," Jasper agreed.

She kissed them each on their cheeks before disappearing in a flash of light.

"Can we join you for the tour?" Grayson asked. "I've never been to another god realm before."

Silas blinked in silence for a moment and then said, "Sure. Just don't attack anyone."

"Do we need to talk about ... *this*?" I asked softly, my cheeks hot as I looked at the ground.

"Yes, but not yet. We're just glad you're safe and ... alive," Silas said and set his hand on my shoulder. "I thought the worst when they came to me at the guild."

"My face still hurts," Parker said and rubbed his jaw.

"You punched him?" I guessed and failed at hiding a smile.

Silas shrugged, unapologetic. "They let you get kidnapped."

"They didn't *let* me get kidnapped. That demon knocked them out. I was barely able to save them from getting chopped in half."

"Apparently Mom was spying on us and saw it. She said she was impressed," Parker said.

"Come on, let's have our tour and then get these three out of here. They're already sweating," Silas said.

The five of us walked out of the castle I was in and out to a stone courtyard where several corpses hung on poles.

"She rules with an iron fist," Silas said. "I'm glad she wasn't able to find you sooner or she might have just killed you."

It hurt to know that Norma had fled like that, left me while I was dying. She couldn't have saved me, but what if I had died? She couldn't have stayed to say goodbye?

"Do you have seasons here?" Jasper asked and pulled his shirt away from his skin.

"This is the Underworld," Silas explained. He pointed up. "That's a rock ceiling. The light you're able to see around here with is actually from all the lava and not from a sun or other typical light source."

"Wait, what happens if we stay here too long? Will we die?" I asked and felt nervous.

Silas shook his head. "No. Our underworld isn't anything like that. I visit here often because I like the heat."

"So, living people can just come and go as they please?" Grayson asked.

Silas nodded. "Since you're alive and not from here, you can't see the souls, but the dead are all around us."

"Weird," Parker whispered.

"We'll take the exit and I'll show you around my world. There's a doorway right over there," Silas said and pointed to the left where an arch with swirling silver magic stood.

"What's to stop the dead from leaving?" Jasper asked.

"The dead can't leave. Just the living," Silas explained. "The dead are incapable of using the door here."

We stepped through the door and out into a world of sunshine and a cool breeze. We were at the top of a mountain that overlooked a glistening ocean, but instead of being blue, it was black.

"What's wrong with your ocean?" Grayson asked with concern.

Silas laughed. "It's perfectly healthy. Come on, I'll show you."

Demons and humans stared openly at us as we walked down a pathway.

There were a few buildings, some vendors with fruits and vegetables, and even some with jewelry.

As we descended the mountain, we came to a village full of demons and humans living together. I wanted to ask questions, but held my tongue, so I wouldn't say something rude that might upset one of the inhabitants.

Down the mountain we walked and came to a huge building with a statue of a man holding a spear and wearing armor. A man that looked like Silas.

"Is that …"

"Yeah, that's my dad," Silas answered. "This is the temple that his followers come to for their prayers and offerings."

"You definitely look like your dad," Grayson commented.

Silas scoffed. "Just a tad."

The sky rumbled, a dark cloud formed, and then Silas's dad materialized out of the sky and floated down to stand before us. He smiled at Silas. "Hello, Son."

Silas dipped his head. "Father."

He looked over at our group and his eyes zeroed in on me. "Nadia," he said and hugged me.

I was being hugged by a god … and not a Norse one.

He stepped back and held my arms as he looked at me. "I'm glad you've recovered. I was worried when I felt you hemorrhaging after the bond with the demoness was severed. She was clever to hide your magic in a bottle with runes from another pantheon. I never imagined she would be one of my own. Had I known, I would have ripped her from you."

I smiled despite that disturbing image and painful recollection of her having been ripped from me. "Things ended well, so it's okay."

He looked over at the trio and held out his hand. "It's nice to meet Nadia's other mates."

Mates …

"Fucking lightning bolts," I gasped and covered my mouth with my hands. I had not just one, but *four* mates. And they had all saved me. Most surprisingly, they had all *accepted* me.

"What?" Silas asked, his brows furrowed.

"Would you like to tour our home?" Silas's father asked, ignoring my outburst.

"Sir, you didn't tell us your name yet," Grayson reminded him. "It feels rude to not know your name when you're offering us hospitality."

"Names have power, so I won't reveal my true one, but you may call me Ere," he answered.

"It's nice to meet you, Ere," Grayson said and shook his hand.

The other two did the same and I stared gaping at the scene.

Ere opened a portal and we all stepped through, coming to a palace of black stone that had a porch right up to the ocean.

"Why is your ocean black?" I asked.

"It's the rocks, not the water," Ere answered, dipped a cupped hand in the water, and raised it to show that the water was crystal clear in his palm. "I used the same rocks to build my palace."

Bending down, I examined the black stone, noting the magical energy in them. "It feels … good," I whispered.

"Yes, it can hold some magic in it. Another reason I used it," Ere said.

"Come on, you've got to see the inside," Silas said and drew me up to a standing position.

The palace was truly amazing and I found myself unable to stop walking around with my mouth opened.

"We should head back to the guild. I bet Dart is freaking out," Silas said as we all stood and stared out at the ocean.

Now that I knew it was black because of the rocks, it really was gorgeous.

"Yeah, you're probably right," I agreed.

"I have a gift for you," Ere said behind us.

We all turned around and my eyes widened when he held out a wooden box towards me.

29

"Me?"

He smiled and nodded. "Yes, but wait to open it until you're alone, okay?"

Silas's eyes narrowed. "Father …"

Ere waved his hand dismissively. "It's nothing bad. I just want her to open it alone. She can show you all after."

Silas grumbled, but said nothing else.

"Thank you," I said and hugged the box to my chest.

"Take care of my boy, okay? I know he's a handful, but you two will do well together." Ere clapped Silas on the shoulder. "Try to prevent your mate from getting kidnapped again, okay? I don't like letting other gods into my territory, but made an exception this one time."

"Will do," Silas said, stepped back, and bowed to his father. "Thank you for allowing me to bring them to rescue Nadia."

Ere smiled at the brothers and said, "You three are welcome here anytime and Nadia, that goes without saying for you as well."

"Thank you, sir," I said.

"Someday, I hope you'll call me father, but I know that will take time." He winked and snapped his fingers. A portal opened behind us, showing the Golden Alicorn main house with Dart pacing in front of it.

I ran through the portal and Dart immediately hugged me. "Nadia!"

"I'm okay," I told him and hugged him back.

His eyes filled with tears and he sniffled. "I was so scared when the trio came."

"Your fears weren't unwarranted," Silas said as he joined us.

Dart and he embraced and I watched, wide-eyed, as Dart hugged the brothers, too.

"I'm so glad you are all safe," Dart said and sat down on the grass. "Whew." He closed his eyes, tilted his head back, and exhaled harshly. "Tell me what happened?"

"Wait, I want to hear as well," Paolo said as he walked out of the house.

"Actually, can we talk to you first?" Parker asked Paolo.

Paolo frowned, but nodded and held open the door to the house.

"I'm going to go with them," Silas said and looked down at Dart. "Keep an eye on her, okay?"

"You got it," Dart agreed and saluted.

"I'm on guild property," I grumbled. "I'm not going to get in trouble."

"You almost died here, remember?" Dart said.

I groaned and sat down beside Dart, lightly punching his shoulder. "You're not helping." Carefully, I set the box Ere had given me on the ground beside me and lay on my back, letting the sun warm my face. So much had happened in the last several days and it was still hard to accept that not only did I have soulmates, but I was bonded to them. Everything was changed.

The warm sun and scent of grass helped ease some of my stress and I forced myself to not think about the potential negatives at this time. The positive was that I didn't have to give up the trio or Silas, they were mine. All mine.

"You look better," Dart commented. "Like a weight has been lifted from you."

"Well, I did lose a demon and get my powers back," I admitted.

"What!" he screamed.

"Shh," I chastised. "I'll explain it all fully, but I fulfilled my contract with the demoness by killing the demon who had been hunting her, and so she gave me my powers back and is gone."

Dart hugged me tightly, squishing me against the ground, and then pulled back with a huge smile. "You have no idea how happy that makes me to hear!"

Tears built in my eyes and Dart's smile slipped.

"Why are you making her cry?" Silas asked as they all came back outside.

"I-I didn't mean to!" Dart yelled.

I threw my arms around Dart's neck and hugged him. "Thank you, for caring about me, for worrying about me." Dart was my first friend who didn't want something out of our friendship, just wanted to truly be friends.

He patted my back and chuckled. "Thank you for being my friend, Nadia. I know I can be annoying and over the top sometimes."

"Sometimes?" Silas teased.

"Okay, often."

I pulled back to glare at Silas. "Like you're one to talk, mister! You're always over the top."

"Okay, I'm tired of waiting. Tell me everything that happened," Dart ordered us.

We each took turns recounting what happened, filling in the pieces the others didn't know. When Silas explained I was hemorrhaging from losing the bond with Norma, my chest tightened and Dart reached over to take my hand, squeezing it for reassurance.

Would I ever see Norma again? Had she really just abandoned me permanently after everything we had been through?

"Wow, so you really do have four soulmates. That's crazy," Dart said when we'd finished.

"I'm glad you have your powers back," Paolo said. "We felt your pain when the bond broke and were all worried."

"How can you all feel her emotions and pain?" Jasper asked.

Paolo shook his head. "We have no idea."

"Silas, can we leave her with you? We'll go back to the cabin to get all our stuff and then report to our guild," Parker said. "We'll bring your backpack also, since you dropped it when you started fighting the demon."

I stood quickly and felt my heart hammering against my chest. "Um, when will I get to see you again?"

The idea of being away from them for more than a night made me incredibly anxious, which I knew was stupid and I needed to get over that since we'd have to be separated when they went on missions. Maybe it was because of the new bond we'd forged.

Grayson picked me up and hugged me, pressing his nose into my hair at the top of my head. "We'll be back tomorrow, promise."

I hugged him back and drew in his scent. "Okay."

Parker and Jasper hugged me as well and walked out of the front gates.

Silas set a hand on my shoulder and squeezed. "They'll be back tomorrow."

"Right," I said and gave a nod.

"Come on, you probably need a warm shower and a change of clothes after the day you've had," Paolo said and opened the door for me. He gave me a warm smile and added, "Welcome back."

30

Grayson, Parker, and Jasper did come back the next day, but aside from a quick hug, I didn't get to see them.

Silas was also busy helping Paolo prepare for the annual festival the guild participated in. Apparently, Paolo had given him some leeway, because he was working with me and Dart. Now, he needed him to help tie up all the loose threads before the event in two days.

Dart had offered to help them as well, so I was on my own.

Walking down the streets of the city, I browsed through some of the stores, determined to find four perfect gifts, but came up with only growing frustration.

"What's got you glaring so angrily at the ground?" Emily asked.

My head snapped up and I winced in pain. "Oh, uh, hi, Emily."

She chuckled and sat down beside me on the porch of the store I'd just left. "What's up?"

"I'm trying to find gifts for, uh, p-people and can't find

anything that is good enough," I admitted. For some reason, I didn't want to admit to her that I had mates just yet. Not that I was embarrassed, but I was hesitant to spread it around.

"Well, I'm free today, so I could walk around with you and help you look if you want?" she offered.

I smiled wide and nodded. "Yes, please."

"How many gifts are you getting?" she asked.

"Four," I answered immediately and then felt my cheeks warm.

She smirked. "Okay. Well, what about Martha's? Her shop has a bit of everything."

I hadn't even considered Martha's! "That's a great idea," I said, stood, and looped my arm through hers after she stood as well. "You're so smart."

Emily chuckled and we walked down the street, weaving around all the people until we got to Martha's.

There were still quite a few people in the shop despite most preparing for the festival, but it wasn't as many as usual which allowed me to breathe a little bit easier and shop without having a panic attack.

We made it to the third floor and Priscilla smiled at us. "Hey, girls! What brings you here today?"

"Well, Nadia is trying to find gifts for her new mates," Emily answered.

My mouth dropped. "You know!"

She chuckled. "Nothing stays secret in a guild for long. Plus, did you really expect the three guys you've been dating to join the guild and us not guess what was going on?"

"Wait, wait. You have how many mates?" Priscilla asked.

"She has four soulmates. Isn't that crazy? Lucky bitch," Emily grumbled.

I smirked and said, "Well, Dart isn't one of them, so he's still free game for you if you ever work up the courage to go ask him out."

She flushed and turned away.

"Okay, so tell me about these four guys," Priscilla said. "What are their main powers?"

"Well, you know about Silas's powers," I said. "The other three are also demigods, but unlike Silas, they can shift into larger forms and—"

"Wait. Hold on! Silas? Silas! Silas is one of your mates?" she squealed.

I nodded.

"You really are a lucky bitch," she grumbled and then shook her head. "No wonder he never looked at any of us girls in that way. He already had a soulmate and just didn't realize it."

"Um, sorry?" I said softly, uncertain how to proceed.

"I've got the perfect thing for Silas. The others, I'm not so sure since I don't know them. Maybe you could get them all something matching instead? Something to signify your relationship?"

If I got us all something that matched, they'd probably like that. Right? I knew I would. But what should I get them? Something we could wear? Definitely not a ring or something like that. Maybe a cuff of bracer?

"What about this?" Emily asked from across the room.

I walked over to the case she was looking inside and gasped. "It's perfect, Em!" Priscilla was already on her way towards us. "Do you have five of these?" Buying so many would eat away a lot of the savings I had, but they were worth it and I was certain they would all like it.

Priscilla looked inside and a huge smile split her face as she nodded. "I'll be right back."

"Thanks for coming," I whispered to Emily. "You definitely helped me out a lot."

She bumped her shoulder into mine and pink tinged her cheeks. "That's what friends are for. By the way, I'm really glad you aren't leaving the guild. Everyone was worried that you might take Silas and Dart and leave us."

"Dart's not my mate," I said urgently, knowing she had a thing for him.

Her cheeks grew brighter. "I know, but he is your partner, and he would probably follow you to another guild if you left."

"Only because *someone* hasn't admitted that they like him," I said.

She squeaked and looked away from me. "It's not that easy."

I patted her back. "I know. Trust me, I don't know if I ever would have admitted to Silas that I liked him."

Priscilla returned and I stopped talking, feeling uneasy talking about Silas and me in front of her more than necessary. "Here you go," Priscilla said and set five identical wrist cuffs on the counter before me. "These have a spot for you to put a magic crystal and a communication stone." She showed me the two spots. "That way, you have a quick magic top off and a way to contact a teammate to let them know you're in trouble."

"She definitely needs that," Emily mumbled.

"Hey!" I protested, but she was right.

Priscilla and Emily laughed while I just shook my head and paid Priscilla who took pity on me and thankfully gave me a discount.

"Will we see you at the festival?" I asked.

Priscilla smiled wide. "You couldn't keep me away! It's my favorite time of year."

"Well, then I'll see you at the festival!" I said as I waved and left the room.

Emily walked beside me, a mysterious purchase in her arms. "Should we stop and eat on the way back or wait and eat back at the guild?"

"Let's eat at the guild," I said. "Tonight, is roast and it's always super tender."

"The potatoes are my favorite part of the roast!" she exclaimed. "We'd better hurry so it's not all gone by the time that we get there."

Linking arms, we jogged all the way back to the guild.

When we got into the dining hall, I wasn't surprised to see that Jasper, Parker, and Grayson had already made several friends and were surrounded with others laughing and joking with them.

What did surprise me was the way they reacted when they saw me. All three immediately stood, stopping mid-conversation, and walked over to take turns embracing me.

"Where have you been?" Grayson asked and held me at arm's length, looking me over.

"I went shopping since everyone else was busy," I admitted. "I'm fine. I can go out on my own and not get into trouble."

"Rarely," Parker mumbled.

I narrowed my eyes at him. "Maybe I won't give you your present then."

"Wait, you got us presents?" Jasper asked and tried to grab the bag, but I spun away from him.

"You can't have them yet!" I yelled and put Emily between us. "I need to eat first. Then, we have to find Silas and I'll give you your presents then."

"You got us all presents?" Grayson asked.

I nodded and felt my cheeks heat up. "Yeah, I did." I suddenly felt really ridiculous and childish for getting them the gifts. "I, um, need to eat. Talk to you later." Ducking my head to try to hide the blush that I felt burning on my cheeks, I pushed Emily toward the food line.

She smirked at me. "Why are you blushing?"

"Shut up," I muttered and let my hair drop down over my face.

"There you are," Dart said as he dropped an arm around my shoulders. "I feel like I haven't seen you in days."

Although it had only been half a day, I knew that he was feeling clingy due to my near-death experience and my rescue he hadn't been able to take part in.

"How are the preparations going?" I asked as we moved forward and I grabbed some food.

"Everything is pretty much ready! Paolo and Silas are just stressing over minor details because they want every-thing to be perfect." He picked up several plates of food and put them on a tray. "Do you want to go on a mission with me tomorrow? I found an easy one and could use the extra money to spend during the festival."

"Sounds great," I agreed with a nod. "I'm pretty low on money at the moment."

Emily snickered and I elbowed her side.

"We may have to go out without Silas, though, since he's helping with the festival preparations still," he said with a frown. "I know they want us to go out in trios."

"What if I go with you?" Emily asked.

My brows shot up into my hairline as I looked at her and then a huge smile split my face. She was finally making a move!

"That's a great idea!" I agreed. "I think it's a great idea for you to join us."

"Okay," Dart said and smiled at her. "Welcome to the team!"

Her cheeks turned bright red and she quickly hurried away to find a table to eat.

I sat across from her and Dart surprised us both by sitting beside Emily.

She smiled as she ate her food and I wondered how long until she admitted her feelings to him.

"Are you trying to get away from us?" Parker asked as he sat on my right.

Jasper sat on my left and Grayson sat across from me, on Emily's other side.

"Why would I try to get away from you?" I asked around the food in my mouth.

"You didn't come sit with us," Jasper said.

"Because your table was full and you were in a conversation with them. I didn't want to interrupt," I answered.

Jasper put his arm around my waist and whispered in my ear, "Babe, you're our mate. You can interrupt us no matter who we're speaking to. You're the most important person in our world."

My cheeks burst into flames, okay not literally, but it felt like it. "You're such a flirt," I accused.

"He's being honest," Parker said. "No one is more important than you."

Emily sniffled. "Oh my gosh, you guys are so cute. Stop it. Wait, don't stop it. Please continue."

Grayson chuckled as my cheeks burned even hotter.

"What are you doing tomorrow?" Grayson asked.

"We're going on a mission," I answered.

"We are?" Parker asked.

I scowled. "Dart, Emily, and I are."

Grayson scowled. "You're going on a mission without us?"

"You guys are your own trio," I said. "And Silas is busy, so Emily is going to fill in for him."

"But—" Jasper started.

"Just promise to keep the necklace on," Parker interrupted him.

I reached up and touched the necklace I had on. "Okay."

"Parker," Grayson said, but shut up from one look from Parker.

Emily and Dart shared a look before ducking their heads down and shoveling food in like they were starving.

It was obvious that I needed to have a private conversation with them to discuss boundaries.

"How are you feeling?" Jasper asked.

"Good," I answered automatically.

"Nadia," Parker pressed.

Finished eating, I stood. "I have something to take care of. I'll see you guys in a bit."

Before they could stop me, I took my tray to the front and hurried to my room. Once inside, I collapsed on my bed and sighed.

I felt great physically, but my heart still hurt from Norma abandoning me. Should I have expected it? Probably. She was a demon after all, but it still hurt. I thought we had developed a friendship, but clearly, she had just used me.

Someone knocked on my door and though I wanted to hide, I got up and opened it.

"Hey," Silas greeted me with a smile. "Heard you were looking for me?"

"Are you done for the day?" I asked and fidgeted.

His smile disappeared and he said, "I also heard you're going on a mission without me."

I nodded. "Emily is coming."

"I don't like it, but I know I can't stop you. Once you and Dart get something in your heads, you're unmovable."

I smirked. "It's part of our charm."

"Mm, I wonder about that," he mumbled.

"So, um, I did have something to talk about, but I'm not really feeling up to it right now," I admitted.

"No way!" Grayson yelled as he burst into my room, pushing around Silas. "What did we do to make you so mad you don't want to give us our presents?"

"Presents?" Silas asked. He looked down at me. "Y-You got me a present?"

Well, I might as well get it over with. "Okay, everyone get in here and line up," I ordered.

The guys each stood at the end of the bed.

Walking to the bags, I took out the presents and set them on the bed in front of each of the guys.

"So, uh, what are the presents for?" Silas asked, looking nervous as he stared at the bag on the bed.

"It's a present for us becoming mates," I said, my eyes downcast to hide my blush and avoid looking at their expressions. I shouldn't have felt embarrassed, but this was the first time I'd given a guy I liked a gift and it was even harder since there were four of them and I was giving them mate gifts.

They picked up their presents in a weird synchronized move and opened them.

Their eyes widened and each removed the bracers, again in a weird synchronized movement.

"These are beautiful," Jasper commented as he, Parker, and Grayson compared theirs.

They were all the same, since I didn't want them to try to claim I favored one over the other.

"Thank you," Silas said and immediately put his on, though he needed help tying the strings to get it tight on his forearm.

"I love it!" Grayson gave me a huge smile and kissed my cheek. "Thank you.

Each helped each other and they proudly held them up, wide smiles forming.

A relieved exhale whooshed from my lungs as I'd been worried they might not like them.

"I know it's not much, but—"

"A gift is a gift," Parker interrupted. "We'd be happy with a rock you found on the road or a flower braided crown. This … you spent time and effort deciding on these and now we can clearly show we're united. It's more than you realize."

Heat rushed to my face and I fanned it. "How do you always know what to say?"

He pulled me into a hug and kissed me deeply, making me forget my embarrassment quickly.

31

For the tenth time, I checked my appearance, adjusting my dress and the new bracer with a green gem that matched the ones I had given the guys.

"You look great," Emily reassured me as she brushed my hair over my shoulder. "Stop worrying."

"Says the girl who changed her top ten times," I countered with a smirk at her in the mirror.

She flushed and turned away. "None of them were right."

We walked out of her room, down hallways bustling with other members also getting ready to head out, and out to the courtyard.

Our mission had been pretty simple in nature, just catch some pixies causing trouble and tie them up to give to the city guards. The little jerks had been fast and full of mischief, though, throwing things at us and putting trip wires everywhere that had made us all fall flat on our faces at least three times each. After three hours, we'd finally finished catching them and secured them for the guards.

We had all needed a shower after that, but the best part was seeing Emily and Dart smiling at each other and whispering about how fun it had been afterwards. I had a feeling that my partner might be going on more missions with Emily soon.

Dart met us first, smiling wide as he took a turn hugging us each. "You guys look great!"

"Thanks," I replied, while Emily blushed.

"There's our girl," Grayson said as he pulled me into a warm hug.

"We wondered how long you were going to make us wait," Jasper said, stealing me from his brother.

"I wasn't making you wait on purpose," I argued against his chest. Despite accepting we were soulmates and what I was feeling was natural, it still felt weird to crave their touch. I hadn't craved it before, but once we were fully bonded, it was much harder to ignore.

Parker waited for me to turn to him and when he saw my red cheeks, smiled wide and kissed me before hugging me with my face against his chest. "Did you miss us?"

"No," I lied.

"You've only been away from her for a couple of hours," Emily said. "Not much time to miss you."

"We missed her," Parker said and tightened his hold on me.

"Are we ready to go?" I asked and stepped away from the brothers, next to Emily.

All five of them nodded.

"Food time!" Dart shouted and linked arms with me while I linked arms with Emily. "First stop is the meat sticks cart. Second stop for rolls."

"Actually," I said, and extricated myself from between him and Emily, then slid their arms together. "I'm going to have to leave you two to hang out together. I promised Silas that I'd meet him right away and he promised to have food for me."

Dart pouted. "We were supposed to hang out as a troop."

"We will, later," I said. "So, you and Emily get all your yummy treats and then meet in the vendor area so we can check out the items for sale. Deal?"

Emily winked at me and pulled Dart away. "Come on! I'm dying to try the snacks. I heard it's the best food of the year and don't want any of them to sell out."

"Look at you, little matchmaker," Grayson teased and draped an arm around my shoulders. "You're adorable."

"I really did promise Silas I'd make my way to him as soon as possible," I admitted.

"We know. He told us. Our new brother was very adamant that we don't try to hog you today, despite him having to take care of the booth," Jasper answered.

"Brother?" I asked, eyes wide as that was the first time they'd referred to him as such.

"He's a demigod, like us, and your mate, so it only seemed right to bring him into our fold. Plus, Grandpa seems to be fond of him," he explained.

Loki being fond of Silas worried me, but it was better not to think about such matters on a day that was supposed to be happy.

"Okay, let's go," I said, "before I change my mind."

Outside of the guild's compound, the city was bustling with far more people than normal. The guys did a good job of keeping people away from me, ensuring I didn't feel crowded or claustrophobic.

Despite saying I needed to find Silas right away and sending Dart and Emily on their own, I did stop to grab some meat sticks from the first seller I saw. I ate them with complete bliss, almost skipping in my joy.

The three brothers all had their bracers on, which was an additional reason for my happiness.

"Do you want some sweet bread?" Grayson asked as the first hint of the baking deliciousness hit our noses.

I only nodded in reply, since my mouth was still full of meat.

"I'll get some for each of us and meet you at the booth so Silas doesn't get upset," he called over his shoulder as he left us to get into line.

"Get some water, too!" Jasper ordered.

Grayson raised a hand in acknowledgement.

"You guys are pretty awesome sometimes," I admitted. We had to slow down as we got to an especially crowded street.

"You mean all the time," Parker countered.

"Have you attended one of these before?" I asked them.

Both shook their heads.

"It'll be all four of our first times then!" I said with a wide smile. "Silas has attended a few, so not his first time."

A few of our fellow guildmembers walked by and we all nodded or raised hands in acknowledgment.

I had a feeling that being their mate was going to give me much more notoriety than I would have attained on my own, and I wasn't certain I liked that.

No one had really said anything yet, but we were a very

odd group, since I had so many mates, so I was certain people would say something eventually.

Why did I have so many mates? Was there some reason that fate had decided to connect us? Was it a freak accident of magic? We weren't all the same age, so it couldn't have anything to do with when we were born.

"You're scowling now. Where did your mind go?" Parker asked and linked our hands together.

I smiled apologetically. "My mind often goes down bad paths. Sorry."

"Talk to us. Tell us what you're thinking about," Jasper urged me.

I hesitated; I uncertain I should tell them what I thought.

"Please," he whispered.

"I was wondering why magic decided to bind us together and what the reason, if any, could be. Doesn't seem like a good option for you lot to have one mate to share between you all. Makes me wonder if I should try to give some of you up." The last sentence I had meant to be internal, but it had come out instead.

"Don't ever think that," Jasper said and squeezed me. "Never."

"We want this. We know the drawbacks and the potential issues, and we choose to stay with you. Please, don't think about trying to 'free' us. We wouldn't have formed the bond if we didn't want it. Whatever the reason magic gave us this bond, we're glad for it."

"Sorry. I wasn't trying to be a downer. I swear. I didn't mean to say that last bit."

"But you feel that, or you wouldn't have said it. We need

to know how you feel," Jasper said. "Even if we don't like it, it's important that we know how you feel."

I wasn't really sure what to say aside from apologizing again, so I just nodded once and looked down at my feet as we continued to walk.

"What did you do to upset her?" Silas demanded as his boots came into view just in front of my feet. He pulled me away from Parker and tilted my chin up so he could look into my eyes.

"Nothing," I said and shook my head. "They didn't do anything."

"She's thinking negatively," Parker explained.

Silas huffed and shook his head. "Father said that I needed to watch out for this."

A child screeched excitedly nearby as they won a treat from the table where Paolo was providing a game for kids to win candy.

The momentary distraction caused us all to relax.

"Today is not the time to discuss this," Silas said and smiled down at me. "Today, we are going to have a fun time eating, drinking, playing games, and enjoying the festivities. Okay?"

I nodded and returned his smile as his enthusiasm and excitement spread to me. "Okay."

He pushed some hair behind my ear and kissed me lightly on the lips. My body tingled and I pressed closer to him, earning a smile and another kiss.

Paolo waved at us as we walked by and then sent a burst of bright blue magic into the air in an explosion of sparkles that had the nearby kids screeching in delight.

We walked around the guild booths, even played a few

games to try to win prizes, but never won any. Not winning didn't matter, since it was just about spending time together, having fun.

"You look exceptionally beautiful tonight," Silas whispered in my ear while we watched Parker and Jasper throw darts at balloons.

My cheeks warmed. "Thank you."

"Food!" Grayson called as he finally found us, carrying not only meat sticks and water, but also a bag of other treats. "Sorry it took me so long, but I couldn't pass up getting all this stuff on the way."

I took one of the offered meat sticks and hummed happily as I ate the soft, juicy meat. "So good."

"What else you got in there?" Silas asked and peeked into the bag. "Oh! Octopus!" He pulled out a stick with an octopus tentacle wrapped around it, grilled and covered in a dark sauce.

"I've never seen that before," I admitted. I knew what an octopus was, but hadn't seen one in person or eaten one.

"It's good, try it," Silas offered me the one he'd pulled out and took another from the bag to eat himself.

"It is really good," Grayson assured me.

"I don't know, you boys eat almost anything," I said skeptically as I took a bite and chewed. A flavor unlike anything I'd experienced before hit my tongue. The meat was a little chewier than the beef I had been eating, but it was still good. "Oh," I exclaimed and took another bite.

"I think she likes it," Grayson said with a chuckle.

"Hey!" Emily called out as she and Dart met up with us.

"Hello," I said around the octopus in my mouth. "Have you had this before? It's so good. Weird, but so good."

She chuckled. "I forgot you hadn't experienced a lot of things before. Yes, grilled octopus is good."

"Woohoo!" Parker yelled as he won the dart game. He took the offered fluffy, rainbow-colored bear and spun around, holding it out to me. "For my beautiful mate."

My cheeks flushed again, partially because it was so new to hearing them call me that in public, partially because my mouth was full and I couldn't really respond, and largely because I had sauce on my face and a ton of people had turned to see who he spoke to.

Silas wiped my face with a napkin, holding back his laughter by squeezing his lips together.

Grayson took my now empty stick, so I could accept the bear.

Swallowing the food that was in my mouth was hard, but I did it and accepted the bear. "Thank you." No one had ever won me a gift before. Tears pricked my eyes and I hugged the fluffy bear tight against my body. It matched my hair.

Parker hugged me, letting me bury my face into his shirt. "You like it?"

"I've never been given a gift at a festival before," I admitted.

"Well, shit, now I've got to win her something, too," Silas said and walked over to another booth, determination in his eyes.

"I'm going to win you the biggest prize of all!" Grayson said, handed Parker the bag of food, and went to a different booth.

"Just remember, I was first," Parker said and winked at me.

Heat flared along my cheeks hotter than before and I shoved his shoulder playfully. "Naughty."

He draped his arm around my shoulders and we turned to watch each of the guys trying to win prizes for me. It was super cute and my heart felt like it couldn't possibly get any fuller.

Dart joined them in trying to win prizes and I worried he might offer it to me, since I was his partner, but he immediately handed the small stuffed dog he won to Emily. She blushed scarlet red as she whispered, "Thank you."

Parker and I exchanged a smile, watching the two.

With my arms full of stuffed animals, we went to the vendor booths and despite my protests, the guys bought me some additional gifts.

"You never did tell us what Ere gave you," Grayson said as the four of us stood next to a booth Dart and Emily were spending a lot of time in.

"Oh," I said. Pulling my dress up slightly on my left leg to reach the dagger sheath there, I pulled out the ornate dagger and showed it to them. The blade was solid black, the hilt silver with four jewels each with a strange power in them, and some inscription in a language I couldn't read.

Silas held out his hand, his eyes wide. "May I?"

"Can you tell me what it says?" I requested. "I don't know that language."

"It says: Prophesized and Protected. This is the dagger of the savior of our world, Antonia. She was a demigod of unusual power who defeated the then demon king who was trying to enslave humans. Antonia is the reason that demons and humans coexist now. She stopped the war and showed everyone that we had much more to gain by working together. This blade will cut through almost anything and these stones hold magical energy from her. The dagger was created by my father as a gift to her for ending the war and the inscription was added to remind any who saw that she was the one they had prophesized about a millennia before. The protected part indicates he had bestowed his protection to her, so any who would dare harm her would face his wrath."

My mouth dropped open. "Whoa." His letter to me had said that he felt I was most deserving of wielding this blade and that he hoped it protected me in the future, but to find out it was such an epic weapon was surreal. And did it mean he was giving me his protection?

"That's awesome," Parker said as he looked over Silas's shoulder at it.

I took the dagger back from him and put it in the sheath. "I'll have to thank Ere next time we see him."

"The finale is starting!" Emily screeched, grabbed my hand, and pulled me away from the guys and deeper into the crowd towards the railing that lined the lake.

"Finale?" I asked. "What's the finale?"

"That's where each of the guild masters puts on a huge magic display," she explained. "You're going to love it."

The guys made their way to us, lined up behind to provide us some protection from anyone else who might come this way to try to get closer, possibly pushing us harder against the railing. I was glad they'd grabbed a bag to put all of the stuffed animals in, since they had been cumbersome to carry and I kept worrying about dropping them.

The finale started, huge fireworks in the shapes of animals and creatures in bright colors.

Standing there, surrounded by my favorite people, watching this display, my soul felt content … happy. For the first time, I felt like my future was going in a perfectly positive direction and I didn't need to fret about money or food.

This was the joy I had searched for for so long. This was the joy that had me looking forward to the future instead of dreading what tomorrow might bring.

"Thank you," I whispered to all of the gods and beings who had helped me get here.

"You're welcome," Loki said from beside me and draped an arm around my shoulders. "I always knew you'd end up as part of my family."

"You did not," I teased, but leaned into him. "But, I'm still thankful."

"Just remember, my grandsons and you are perfect matches. So, whatever happens in the future, it's okay to depend on them."

I nodded and looked over my shoulder at them and Silas. "I know. For the first time, I know I can count on others."

He patted my arm and winked at his grandsons. "Enjoy your festival."

He disappeared in the next instance, but the feeling of completeness only grew.

My happily ever after was here and I was going to do everything I needed to ensure it stayed.

32

BONUS: MISSION OF THE THIEVING PIXIES AND WHY YOU SHOULDN'T WEAR WHITE DURING MISSIONS

"Pixies don't usually steal things," I whispered as we crawled towards the edge of the rooftop. "Cause mayhem and move things around, yes, but not steal things."

"That's what the mission request said," Silas whispered back. "And that's why we're doing recon first, before jumping straight in to try to capture them."

Peering over the edge of the rooftop, I watched as a woman deliberately set a couple pastries nestled on parchment paper on her windowsill, like one might do to wait for them to cool. She also set another pastry on a beautiful silver platter.

Across the street from her, another woman *accidentally* dropped the key to her front door on the porch as she stepped inside the house, shutting and locking the door behind her.

Dart and Emily sat at a table outside the pub, chatting and looking like normal citizens. They looked like a couple on a date, which might not be far from the truth. Dart wore his normal leather pants and boots, but today he wore a white shirt with an open collar and puffy sleeves. I had never seen the shirt before, but had to admit that it was nice looking and added to the lie that they were on a date. Emily wore her normal trousers and knee-high boots as well as a regular brown shirt, but over that she wore a vest that was almost corset-like with laces up the front. It accentuated her bustline and I wanted one for myself.

Parker, Jasper, and Grayson were in the pub, chatting it up with the locals and drinking, to prepare for their act of drunken idiots stumbling through the streets as bait.

Now, we just had to wait.

Silas folded arms in front of him, on the very edge of the roof, and lay his head sideways on them so he could look at me. "So, how are you feeling?"

"Tired of answering that," I answered truthfully. Each of the guys asked me individually at least twice a day. It had been two months since we'd become fully bonded and I'd accepted that I had not just one, but four soulmates.

"We just want to be sure that you're doing okay and if you need anything, to handle it."

"Can you stop my cramps, because that would be great," I teased.

He smirked. "We can totally do that. You see, when a woman is pregnant …"

My face felt like it was engulfed in flames as I looked away from him. "Incorrigible."

His soft laughter eased some of my embarrassment. It was good to hear him laugh, something he'd been doing more since the brother trio had come into our lives.

"I'm not really sure about kids," I admitted as I looked back at him. Fortunately, a store near the guild had medicine to ensure I didn't end up pregnant until I was ready. Unfortunately, I still had my monthly flows and cramps.

He smiled sweetly. "We aren't rushing you or going to force you. If you don't want kids, that's fine, but if you end up wanting them you only have to ask."

"How are you feeling?" I asked back, partially to get the focus off of me and partially because I was curious.

"Pretty good," he said, though his smile wilted a little. "I'm still getting used to having them around all the time, but they're fun and easy to be around, which helps. Plus, they don't try to hog you, which I was worried might happen."

"So, no jealousy?" I asked.

He scoffed. "Oh, plenty of jealousy, but I know they're your other soulmates, so it's easier to accept and learn to live with."

"Do … do you ever wish you hadn't become my soulmate?" I asked softly. "If you had found someone who would be with just you and you alone, so you wouldn't have to share."

"I don't want a different woman," he said immediately and scooted closer to me so he could kiss my forearm, since it was the closest thing to him. "Would it be nice to have you to myself? Yes, but we can work that out between the four of us. Maybe we can discuss stealing you away for individual dates?"

"Individual dates sounds nice," I admitted.

Any date sounded nice. We'd been busy with missions and rebuilding the house that had been destroyed by the White Chimeras' attack.

"You got that scowl-y look on your face. What are you thinking?"

It was now or never. Time for me to take initiative for the things I wanted. "Will you go on a date with me in two days?" I asked. "Or, at least two days after we finish this mission?"

His eyes widened a moment before he nodded and smiled. "I would love to."

I leaned over and he met me halfway, kissing me on the lips. He carefully moved until he lay with his upper body on mine, deepening the kiss even more. Our tongues danced and I lost myself to his hands on my face and the kiss.

After an unknown amount of time, he pulled back and stroked his thumb across my now swollen lips. "I am an incredibly lucky man."

"If you play your cards right, you could get even luckier tonight," I said, suddenly feeling bold.

His eyes widened and he kissed me again. "Stop teasing me while we're on a mission. We might miss something."

I laughed as he took his place back beside me. Movement down below caught my eye. Pointing, I got him to focus back on the mission and the little pixies who had been causing issues.

Four tiny humanoid creatures with wings, clawed fingertips, and sharp teeth flew down low, hiding along planter boxes and carts to stay hidden as the sun set. Two were bluish, one was a pretty pink, and one was red like blood.

Keeping completely still, Silas and I watched them, waiting for them to act the way the townspeople had indicated, to prove that they were more than just mischief makers.

One of the blue pixies crawled up the side of the house beneath the open window where the pastries lay, darting its head back and forth to ensure no one noticed. It reached the windowsill and sat very still, its head tilted slightly to the side with its ear to the window, listening for the movement of the owner inside.

To my complete surprise, the pixie took the silver tray, but put the pastry from that tray next to the others on the parchment paper, ensuring it rested in exactly the same way.

It really was stealing!

My muscles tensed, wanting to jump down now and grab them, but we needed to watch them a little longer, to see if it was all four of them or just this naughty ringleader.

Grayson, Parker, and Jasper stumbled out of the bar, laughing and slapping each other on the back as they veered across the small street. I could smell the booze on them from here! When we discussed them going into the pub to drink to come out and act drunk, I'd expected them to simply *act*, not get drunk!

The pink and red pixie chittered to each other and zoomed forward. With a speed that was impressive, they untied the trio's boots and then tied them so they were all interlaced together.

Immediately, all three men fell to their hands and knees.

The sun fully set and the two pixies flew into a dark corner, chittering with laughter as they hid.

"Damned pixies," Parker grumbled as they worked to untie their boots.

The second blue one that had so far only watched its friends now moved to the dropped key.

It grabbed the key, put it into the lock, and opened the door.

"Get them!" I hissed to Silas, but he was already dropping down, headed for the blue pixie breaking into the house with the dropped key.

That was unacceptable behavior, especially since it could have just flown into the cracked open window instead of unlocking the door and opening it for a more dangerous creature or person to come inside and potentially harm the family.

While Silas went after that one, I went after the silver platter thief.

The pink and red pixies flew back towards their friends, shrieking loudly when they noticed us trying to capture them.

I got the bag over the blue thief, forcing it to drop the silver platter, but with unexpected strength and speed, it pulled me by the bag towards the table Dart and Emily sat at.

I yelped in surprise as it dragged me along and ended up hitting the table with my upper torso, knocking the table over onto Dart.

Tea, jam, and water splashed all over his shirt, turning it from white into a tie dye experiment.

The pixie laughed, enjoying the spectacle, but I tightened my grip on the bag and sealed it closed with a magical tag. "Laugh all you want, but you're mine."

Jasper and Grayson suddenly exploded into their giant forms, reaching out and snagging the pink and red ones respectively in huge fists.

Silas joined us, the other blue one in his bag, screeching and hissing at him.

Jasper and Grayson put theirs in a bag and shrunk back down.

"Mission accomplished," I huffed.

Dart wiped at his shirt, but it was definitely ruined.

"That is why you don't wear white on missions," I told him with a smirk.

He stuck his lower lip out in a pout and said, "I liked this shirt."

"Well, go and buy it in black, then," Silas suggested.

Everyone laughed as Dart mimicked him, and we went off to find the mayor to collect our pay for completing the mission.

33

BONUS: MISSION OF THE SEXY SIREN AND WHY SOULMATES ARE THEIR ENEMIES

Five months after Norma was removed, I received a single letter from her. It was an apology, but with no return address or anything else. I supposed that was all the closure I would get the from the demoness. I had just been a means to an end for her, after all.

"You look annoyed," Parker commented as he met me in the dining hall. "Want to go on a mission to work some of that out?"

I nodded vigorously, swallowing my food quickly. "Yes, please."

His eyes lit up with amusement. "Wonderful. I already have one picked out. Go grab your gear."

After finishing my drink, I put the dishes in the tub by the door and hurried to my room. Changed, geared up, and backpack on, I met the trio at the front door.

"Ready," I said and pushed open the doors.

"Have fun!" Dart called out as he walked through the entryway and waved.

I waved back. "Take Emily out while I'm gone."

His cheeks turned red, but he smiled and nodded. "Good idea."

Jasper reached over and grabbed my hand, interlocking our fingers together as we walked off the guild property, into town, and towards the portal center.

"Do you want to talk about why you're upset? Was it one of us?" Jasper asked softly.

Exhaling harshly, I tried to rid myself of the anger, but it didn't work. "Norma sent me a letter apologizing for everything. No return address or anything else."

His hand tightened around mine. "I'm sorry. Do you want us to try to find her? I'm pretty sure Silas could ask his dad or maybe even find her himself. We didn't realize you were wanting to find her."

Of course they hadn't, since I hadn't told them.

"I don't know anymore," I admitted. "I wanted to find her, to see her and talk to her, but she's clearly moving on with her life and I suppose I should as well." I looked up at him and said, "You know we never took that three day trip like we'd discussed. The one to celebrate our bonds. Maybe we could do that soon?"

We stopped, now in line for the portals.

He rested his hand against my cheek and I leaned into it. "If you want to take a trip, just the five of us, we'll set it up."

I nodded. "Yes, please."

"Do you want to go back to the lake?" Parker asked behind me.

I turned and looked at him. "Is it still snowy?"

They all shook their heads.

Grayson said, "It's spring time there, so it'll be really pretty and the lake will be cold, but not frozen."

"That sounds amazing," I said. "We just have to clear the time away with Paolo and make sure Silas is up for it."

"Oh, Silas will be up for it. Trust me," Grayson said and pulled me away from Jasper and into his arms. "We've all been dying to get you away from everyone, alone, and someplace we can really let loose and have fun with you."

"Someplace you won't be embarrassed about being too loud," Jasper whispered in my ear as he ran his hands up and down my arms.

Heat flared in my lower stomach and I squeezed my legs together. "Boys," I said breathily, "you're going to end up causing a scene that Paolo will chastise us for and the public will be appalled by."

All three laughed and took a step back from me.

No longer in the cocoon of warmth, I was hit with a cold wind that allowed me to breathe a little easier. I took out my water flask and drank some to help further cool my body, though my mind was still racing with thoughts of them and what it would be like to have them all together. Since we were all staying at the main house, I usually slept in one of their rooms, but the beds weren't meant to be shared, so I only slept with them one at a time. And they were right, I was constantly worried about being too loud and one of the other guild members hearing us.

Would Silas be willing to … participate with them or would he only want to have time with me alone?

The trio had mentioned they had shared a woman before, but our circumstances so far had prevented me from experiencing that. It was definitely something I wanted to try.

"Our turn," Jasper said, pulling me out of my thoughts.

Just as I reached for my coins, Jasper paid for all of us instead.

"Grayson first, then Nadia. Parker, bring up the rear," Jasper ordered.

Was he worried we might get attacked when we walked through?

As I stepped through, I realized I hadn't even asked about the mission or where we were going. I trusted them, so that wasn't an issue, but I probably should have asked.

On the other side of the portal, I opened my eyes and gasped. A beautiful blue sea glistened before me, birds cried out overhead, and massive ships bobbed in the water over colorful coral reefs. The docks were full of people bustling about. I had been to ocean cities before, but never to this one. Turning, I could see a couple warehouses farther down the waterline and beyond that was the town, full of colorful buildings and narrow cobblestone streets that lead to the docks. This had to be Port Crescendo. A bustling port town with an enchanted bay, where ships can dock among the colorful coral reefs while they unloaded and loaded cargo. There was an abundance of brightly colored street vendors selling their wares and enchanting music that could be heard from the nearby tavern. This Por was known for its great markets and powerful fleet. Beyond the port and city stood three towers of shining glass and crystal, the confirmation that it was indeed Port Crescendo. The towers looked ostentatious, but were enchanted to withstand even an explosion.

Grayson grabbed my arm gently and tugged me to the side so Jasper wouldn't bump into me when he walked through.

"We could delay our mission another day to give us some time to sightsee," Grayson suggested. He wrapped his arms around me, standing with his chest pressed into my back.

"What is our mission?" I asked just as Jasper walked through.

"There are some naughty sirens pulling sailors from their ships and eating them," Jasper answered. "Our job is to convince them to leave or kill them if they won't listen."

My mouth dropped. "You saw a job posting for a siren, luring men to become meals, and thought it would be a great idea for *three men* to take the job? Are you insane?"

"They won't be able to tempt us," Grayson said and tightened his hold on me.

"I admire your conviction, but these are sirens. All the lore I have ever read says that only straight women are immune to their calls. I understand why you asked me to go on the mission, but you should have had me come with Emily instead of bringing you three. You're like a ... prime buffet for them!"

Jasper laughed while Parker smiled.

"We're glad you can admit to us being prime choices amongst men," Parker said.

I groaned and stepped away from Grayson to rub a hand down my face. "Seriously, what are you three thinking taking on this job? They are sirens. You are men."

"That's why you need a capable crew of women to help on this job," a throaty female voice said behind me. The orc looked to be a smug female with thick tusks jutting from her lower jaw. She had a wide, flat nose and small, beady eyes. Her skin was a greenish-grey, and her body was muscular and stocky. She's also looked quite strong, and likely wasn't afraid to use her fists to get what she wanted. She wore a tan tunic and brown trousers with a belt full of knives and a cutlass at her hip. She smelled like sweat and stale ale, and she looked like she was ready, no wanting a fight.

"Name's Grul'ma," she introduced herself and held out a thick hand.

"Nadia," I replied as I gripped her hand to shake it.

Jasper stepped forward and held out his hand. "I'm Jasper, Nadia's mate. These are Grayson and Parker, also her mates."

Grul'ma's eyes widened. "I've heard of someone with multiple soulmates before, but never thought I'd see them in person."

"She's got one more, but we left him at home," Grayson said with a smirk I couldn't comprehend.

"Damn girl, what god did you pray to to get so lucky?" Grul'ma asked and laughed as she nudged her shoulder against mine. "I'm just razzin' you! Are you wanting to get on the ship and sleep there tonight?"

"We'd actually like to look at the ship, but we're going to stay at the inn tonight," Parker answered quickly.

She nodded. "Sounds good. I'd rather not scrub puke out of the cabins any more than I have to." With a laugh and another nudge of her shoulder against mine, she led the way to the ship, which was apparently on the far side of the docks.

"She's not particularly intelligent, but she is cunning and manipulative. Don't let her fool you," Parker whispered while Grayson chatted with the orc.

"I'll keep that in mind," I said, though I wondered if she was smart and pretended otherwise so people underestimated her.

"You're still tense," he commented and linked his hand with mine.

"I'm worried about you three being lured by sirens," I reminded him.

"Baby, they aren't going to be able to lure us," he said softly and kissed my cheek as we walked. "Trust us."

"I do, but I'm still going to be worried," I said. How could they resist a siren's call? Maybe I should shackle them to the ship to ensure they didn't jump off? Would Grul'ma have shackles on the ship?

We walked around the ship, the guys investigating it for what I had no idea.

"You have shackles on here?" I asked Grul'ma.

She smiled wide. "Oh, you're anticipating having that kind of fun on board, are you?"

My cheeks warmed and I shook my head. "No, it's not that!"

"The lady doth protest too much," Grayson teased and put his arm around my waist.

"Gray," I growled.

"Oh, she's feisty! I knew I liked you," Grul'ma said and laughed more. "I do have some shackles, but I'm certain they won't hold these three. Not when they can go giant size and just snap the cuffs."

"Wait, you've worked with them before?" I asked.

She nodded. "We've had lots of fun." She winked at Parker, who smiled in response.

Jealousy reared its head, but I squashed it down. There was no need for that now. Whatever the past was, was just that … the past.

"Wait, if you already worked with her, why did you introduce yourselves?" I asked Jasper.

Grul'ma smiled. "I don't remember their names. Once I'm done with them, they float off on the breeze like a leaf." She waved her hand like a leaf floating.

Laughter burst out of me and I clutched my stomach as it hurt from laughing so hard.

"Alright, get off my ship and go get a room at the inn. We leave at dawn, so don't be late!"

We waved to her as we left and I followed behind Jasper and Grayson as they led the way to the inn.

"Why aren't we leaving tonight?" I asked over my shoulder to Parker.

He jerked his eyes up, having been looking at my butt. "Ships aren't supposed to leave at night because it's easier to hit the coral or each other with the low lighting."

"Aren't sirens nocturnal?" I swore I had read something about them being nocturnal or maybe luring beings more often when it was dark.

"They prefer hunting at night, but since hunting is harder for them in general, they hunt at all times of the day. From what we've learned, they hunt in packs with half hunting at night and half hunting during the day," he answered.

"Wow, you're not just a pretty face after all," I teased.

He grabbed me and tickled me. "Come here. You're such a brat sometimes."

Squirming was fruitless, but I still tried to escape his tickles, squealing with laughter.

"Isn't this an adorable sight," a deep male voice grumbled and spit to the side.

"It is, so why are you ruining it? Move along," Parker snapped and pushed me behind him.

Before he pushed me behind him, I got a chance to look at the speaker, but didn't recognize him. The older man looked quite angry, and it seemed that much of his ire was directed at Parker. He had a wild look in his eyes, and his long, grey hair was unkempt. He was dressed in dark colors with a hooded cloak that had a broach with a symbol I didn't recognize. While he may have been older, his magic seemed strong, swirling around him, and he was not to be underestimated.

"You three think you're hot shit because you're demigods. Well, let me tell you something, demigods are a dime a dozen here. You aren't any more special than the botfly on my horse."

"We get it, you're intimidated by us and you're trying to make me look bad in front of the woman I'm with. Sorry, Larry, but it's not working and we've got things to do. So, if you'll excuse us?" Parker pulled me after him and I got a chance to see the guy's face again.

He was fuming, literally smoking from his fingertips. "Fuck you!"

Whatever he was planning to do, I wasn't going to let it happen. I released half of my power, my hair glowed, casting rainbows everywhere, and I stepped right into his personal space. "You, sir, need to go have a drink and calm down." I put two coins in his hand.

The magic he had been gathering disappeared as he gaped at me.

I turned my back on him, contained my magic, and dragged a smiling Parker away, so he couldn't say anything stupid to restart the fight between them.

Jasper and Grayson had smug smirks on their faces as we met up with them at the entrance to the inn.

"What?" I asked.

"You're sexy when you get protective," Jasper whispered, grabbed me, dipped me, and kissed me deeply.

"Get a room!" an old woman growled as she walked by.

"We're working on it," Parker replied back in a playful tone.

Jasper straightened and I clung to him, my mind reeling from the kiss and not quite able to stand on my own yet.

Grayson pushed open the door and ushered us all inside.

"Evening, friends. What can I do for you?" a spindly man with wire-rimmed glasses and a kind smile greeted us.

"Two rooms, please," Grayson requested.

"We have a reservation," Parker reminded him.

"Oh, right. Two rooms under the name Helson," Grayson amended.

"Here you are," the clerk said. "You lucked out in getting the last set of adjoining rooms." Turning behind him, he grabbed two keys from the wall and set them on the desktop. "Looks like your guild paid for the room in advance as well."

The guild had paid for it?

We hurried upstairs to the rooms and after a few bouts of ro-sham-bo, Parker took my hand and pulled me into one of the rooms. It had a large bed and a view of the docks.

Staring out at the water, I couldn't help, but feel apprehensive about the upcoming mission. Sirens against three demigods.

"Why are you worried?" Parker asked, stepped up behind me, and slid his arms around my waist.

"Once they lure you, I won't be able to stop you. You'll go giant and toss me to the side like a doll."

He set his chin atop my head and shook his head. "They won't be able to lure us, love."

"You three should stay here and let me and Grul'ma handle this mission," I said and spun to look up at him.

He cupped my face and kissed my lips lightly. "Forget about the mission for now. Let's go get some food and walk around the town. We've got some time before the sun sets."

Arguing with him right now would be pointless, so I would hold my tongue until tomorrow morning.

"Food does sound good," I agreed, shoved his chest with my hands as hard as I could so he fell onto the bed, and smirked. "But I don't think we are ready yet for dinner."

His frown turned into a smile. "What did you have in mind, mate?"

I closed the curtain over the window, pulled my shirt off over my head, and turned around to face him. "I think we need to work up an appetite before we eat."

He reached back and with one pull removed his shirt

from over his head, revealing a chiseled body that never failed to make me drool.

Grayson pushed open the door and asked, "Are you ready for dinner?" His mouth hung open when he saw me standing in my bra and pants.

"Move," Jasper ordered him, pushing into the room, but immediately stopped once inside and he could see me. "Shut the door, Gray."

Grayson shut the door behind him and locked it without turning around, his eyes fixed on me.

"Nadia thinks we should work up an appetite before we go find dinner," Parker informed them.

Grayson nodded. "Sounds like a great idea to me."

"A perfect plan," Jasper said and pulled his shirt off.

The room wasn't very large to begin with and with three demigods, it was even smaller. I wasn't really sure how to coordinate any of this, since we hadn't had a group session yet. But I figured the guys would guide me, so I just finished undressing.

They finished as well, presenting me with three perfect male specimens to appreciate and enjoy.

"Nadia," Parker said softly, getting my attention on him. He crooked his finger. "Come here, beautiful."

Obeying, I walked up to him where he now sat on the side of the bed, his legs spread so I could stand between them.

He ran his hands up the backs of my legs, over my butt, and gripped my hips. Before I realized what he was doing, he spun and tossed me onto the bed.

Grayson dropped to his knees and claimed my mouth with his.

Jasper leaned over on the bed, his tongue circling one nipple and then the next.

Parker dropped to his knees and buried his face in me, licking and sucking and making me moan into Grayson's mouth.

So many hands and mouths on me at once was overwhelming, but also *so* good.

Parker slid two fingers inside of me, pumping in and out as his tongue licked up and down.

My scream of ecstasy was swallowed by Grayson and my hips bucked up as I orgasmed. Grayson pulled back and smiled. "Oh, yeah, baby. Just like that."

"More," I panted.

And my handsome trio obliged without hesitation.

After a quick trip to the washroom to clean up, we headed down to the pub for dinner. Smiling like an idiot and unable to stop, I sat next to Jasper, holding his hand beneath the table.

"Drink?" Jasper asked.

I nodded. "Sure."

Grayson waved down one of the workers and gave our order for food and drinks. I trusted them so I didn't even pay attention to what they ordered, much more interested in looking around at the patrons.

The great thing about port cities like this was the variety of beings who visited. Humans, orcs, fae, shapeshifters, and so many more filled the pub. They laughed and shared food and drink together as well as swapping stories and experiences.

I had always dreamed of moving to a city like this, somewhere that would let me meet a variety of people.

An older orc couple leaned across a small table, rubbing their noses together as they whispered. It was adorable.

"Looking forward to getting old?" Jasper asked.

I snorted and shook my head. "No, not at all. Although, knowing I'll have you guys with me definitely makes it more appealing." A worrisome thought popped into my head and I felt my brows furrow.

"What?" Grayson asked.

"You guys age different than humans or gods, being demigods, right?" I asked.

All three nodded.

"Does that mean …" Would I die before them? Would I age while they stayed young?

"Uh oh, what are you thinking? Spit out the full question," Parker said and leaned his elbows on the table as he stared at me, waiting.

Spitting out the question seemed the best idea. "Am I going to die before you?"

Grayson and Parker jerked back, eyes wide.

"Wh-What?" Grayson asked.

"I'm human," I whispered and looked down at my hand in my lap. "I'm going to age faster than you."

Jasper's hand tightened around mine as he, Grayson, and Parker exchanged scowling expressions.

"We would need to talk to –"

"Hello, children. I heard your call," Loki said as he

pulled up a chair to our table, joining us. He looked over at me and smiled wide. "Well, don't you look … satisfied."

"Loki," I growled.

"Why did you summon me?" he asked Parker.

Parker scowled. "I didn't mean to."

Loki waved his hand dismissively. "I'm here. Out with it, child."

"Nadia is worried because we are all demigods, but she's only human," Grayson said quickly. "Is she right? Is she going to age faster than us and die before us?" Grayson's chest heaved at the end, his worry clear.

Reaching across the table, I held my hand out and he immediately took it, clenching mine as he waited for Loki to speak.

Loki looked at me, squinted his eyes, and looked back at Parker. "She's not a normal human."

"Excuse me?" I asked, feeling somewhat offended.

"I don't know about her aging capabilities, but she doesn't …" He waved his hand at me like that explained anything. "… she's not like normal humans when I inspect her. We can keep an eye on her aging over the next decade and if things look … dire, we can figure out a course of action then."

"Course of action?" I asked.

"Will we age the same as Silas? Does it matter what pantheon you come from?" Grayson asked.

Loki frowned and looked up at the ceiling. "I'm actually not certain, but I can't see why one pantheon's demigods would age differently than another's. Again, we can track that over the next ten years and see."

"I don't want to live hundreds of years without her,"

Jasper whispered, grabbed me, and pulled me into his lap, nuzzling against my throat.

"I won't let that happen," Loki assured him. "Even if extreme measures need to be taken, I will assist you."

Jasper said, "Mom doesn't want us to upset the balance of –"

"Who said your mom has to be involved?" Loki replied immediately, interrupting him.

"Loki, do you know what mission they accepted?" I asked from within Jasper's arms.

"No, care to enlighten me?"

"Loki, they're wanting to face sirens! Why would your three grand*sons* think it was okay to face off against sirens?" I scoffed at the end thinking he would agree it was as ridiculous as I made it sound.

"Oh, it's fine," he said. "I'll see you later. Have a good night."

Before I could speak again, he disappeared.

"What the heck?" I whispered. How was he not on my side either about the insanity of them facing sirens?

"Jas, let her go," Parker ordered.

Jasper growled, nuzzled my neck once more, but reluctantly released me so I could sit back in my own seat.

"I'm worried now and he didn't put me at ease at all," Jasper growled.

"He said he'll help in any way he can," I reminded him.

"Not good enough," he growled. His body started to shake, but after Grayson set his hand on Jasper's shoulder, it stopped.

"Well, after I lose you to the sirens, it won't matter." I scoffed and flipped my hair over my shoulder.

The waitress brought our drinks over and I chugged half of mine quickly. Stubborn men would be the death of me.

"Hello, boys," a woman purred as she sauntered up, her cleavage barely contained by her shirt. She looked to be middle-aged with long, curly red hair that shone brightly even in the dim room.

"Darla," Grayson said, and dipped his head in greeting.

"In town for another mission?" she asked, twirling some of her hair around her finger.

"Yes," Parker answered.

"How long will you be in town? I'm available if you need some … entertainment."

"They've got plenty of entertainment already," I said as cheerfully as I could, though even I heard the bite to my tone.

Her eyes fell on me, she took a long look at me, scowled, and shrugged. "You know where to find me when you're ready for some *real* entertainment."

"Deep breath," Jasper ordered me.

"Stupid women throwing themselves at my men," I grumbled and took another gulp of my drink.

"You're adorable when you're jealous," Grayson said and leaned his chin atop of fists on the table, batting his eyelashes like a fool.

"Do you guys have a gameplan for the sirens?" I asked instead of acknowledging his statement or my jealousy.

"Yes," Jasper said. "We're going to play bait and when they come to the ship, we'll politely ask them to stop killing people here. If they refuse, then we'll resort to less polite requests."

"And why would they leave such a prime hunting ground peacefully?" I asked.

Jasper smiled. "They'll acknowledge that living, but going to another hunting area is better than dying and no longer being able to hunt."

I highly doubted he was right, but I had my fingers crossed that's how it would go down.

"Your food," the waitress said. She looked at my empty cup and her lips twitched. "Care for another?"

I nodded. "Please."

She winked. "I'll bring back two."

"Bless you," I breathed and finally looked at the food. It was a huge piece of roast with potatoes and carrots on the side.

I clearly hadn't realized how hungry I'd been as I devoured my entire plate before she returned with my drinks.

"Do you want more food?" Jasper asked.

I shook my head and started sipping on my new drink. "No, I'm good."

"You sure?" Grayson asked.

I nodded. "I'm full now."

"Must have done something fun to work up that level of appetite," the waitress said, winked, and laughed as she headed off to deal with other tables.

The trio resumed their eating, releasing me to once again look around the room. A fight started between two male orcs and just as I opened my mouth to warn the guys, one of the orcs flung a chair away from them, right at us.

Hopping up out of my seat, I grabbed the chair, spun in

a circle, and threw it back at the orc. It smacked into his head and broke apart.

"Whoops," I said, since I hadn't meant to hit him with it, just toss it back over there.

The orc snarled as he turned to face me, blood dripped from his face.

"We can't take you anywhere," Jasper teased me.

The angry orc roared and stomped towards me. Jasper, Grayson, and Parker stood and stepped between us, stopping the orc before he could reach me.

"Sorry, our mate has a bit of a temper," Jasper apologized. "You can return to your fight over there."

"My fight is here now," the orc snapped and swung a fist at Jasper.

Grayson grabbed the orc's arm, stopping his fist just before it could hit Jasper. "That's not very nice, sir. We're just trying to enjoy a meal."

"You should have trained your bitch to act better then," the orc snarled.

Grayson's brows furrowed and he punched the orc in the face, knocking him across two tables behind him.

The people at the tables' food and drink covered their laps. They looked up at Grayson and the orc and within seconds, an all-out brawl started.

Jasper and Parker stayed at my sides, punching and pushing away anyone that got too close to me.

"This definitely wouldn't have happened if Silas were here," I teased.

"Only because he follows the rules all the time," Jasper said.

"I'm so glad you guys aren't squares," I said.

Grayson knocked out the orc finally and made his way over to us. "We should probably leave."

I nodded my agreement and together they forced their way out of the tavern, paying the waitress as we walked by her at the door.

She winked at me and said, "Have a good night."

After walking around a bit, we went to bed, since we had to get up early. I slept with my head on Grayson's chest and it was one of the best sleeps I'd ever had.

"You look like you had a good night," Grul'ma commented as we boarded her ship.

Several women walked around the boat doing various tasks, preparing for us to sail.

"I did," I agreed with a wide smile. A cold wind blew and I rubbed my arms against the chill.

"I told you we should have gotten her a better coat," Jasper said, came up behind me, and wrapped his arms around me.

"I'm fine," I assured him.

"Let's sail!" Grul'ma bellowed.

Her crew leapt into action, moving about the ship and doing things that I had no idea about.

"Let's get out of their way," Parker said, took my hand, and led me up to an upper area where the wheel to steer the ship was and a great view.

The coral sparkled in bright colors, visible through the crystal clear water.

Grul'ma came up behind us, taking the wheel.

"How long will it take to get to the area the sirens were last reported at?" Grayson asked.

"Not sure. Hopefully no more than half a day," she answered.

The ship headed away from the docks and out to the open ocean.

A mixture of excitement and anxiety filled me. I'd never been out in the open ocean before. Truthfully, it was a little frightening when I thought about all the creatures that called the ocean their home and could devour me in a single gulp.

Holding onto the railing, I watched the water we glided over and the fish and other creatures I could see in the depths below. It was a whole other world down there.

"You okay?" Parker asked, his words whispered into my ear.

I nodded. "I've never been out here before. It's beautiful."

"You're beautiful," he whispered and placed a kiss against my neck just below my ear.

Tilting my head back so I could look at him, I smiled. "Thank you for taking me on this mission."

His fingers caressed my cheek. "I'd do almost anything for you, Nadia."

"Almost anything?"

His lips twitched. "I have a few hardlines, but they're very few."

"Like?"

"I won't ever give you up," he whispered and kissed me tenderly.

"You're so sweet, it's giving me a toothache," I said.

He laughed and nuzzled his nose behind my ear. "Only for you, baby. Only for you."

I had worried the movement of the ship would make me queasy, but I actually enjoyed the sway.

We sailed for hours, occasionally passing other ships, but it was mostly empty, open water for as far as you could see.

After almost half a day, we found a tiny island with three beautiful women. The island was so small, it barely fit the three of them lying down. They wore shell and seaweed tops and had gorgeous multicolored scales starting just below their belly buttons and morphed into a tail.

They perked up when they saw Grayson, Jasper, and Parker at the front.

"Hello, boys!" the women called out.

Grayson, Jasper, and Parker raised their hands and waved.

"We've come to tell you that you need to leave and find a new hunting ground," Jasper called out to them.

The three women looked at each other and cackled with laughter. The center one shook her head. "Silly men. We aren't going anywhere." She smiled, showing teeth similar to a shark's.

The other two started singing, no words, just notes, and the magic they used made the hairs on my arms stand up.

I prepared to restrain the guys. There was no way I was going to let these sirens take them.

"We're asking nicely because we don't want to hurt you," Grayson said loud enough they could hear over their singing.

The two women stopped their song, looked at the

middle one, and some silent communication passed between them.

As one, they all started singing. "Come away with us, handsome man. Come play in the surf with us, have some fun. Let us take away your worries. Enjoy your time with our bodies."

Grayson, Jasper, and Parker jumped up onto the railing.

I drew my sword and let my magic out, the rainbows showing on the deck and reflected in the water. "They're not going near you."

"Wait," Grul'ma said suddenly and grabbed my arm. "Look at your men."

Harming the woman who could sail us back to land wasn't a smart decision, so I looked at them. To my surprise, they didn't look bewitched. They looked … pissed.

The trio jumped from the ship to the island. Their bodies grew to their giant sizes and the sirens started to move closer to them. Their song grew louder, as did their smiles.

"We asked nicely and now we're going to be mean," Parker said, his black hair waved behind him like a flag and reminded me of a battle mural painting I'd seen in Asgard.

"Th-They're not affected by the sirens?" I asked softly.

"You're soulmates. They won't be swayed by another woman, even a siren," she said. "I thought you knew that."

"That's why I asked about the cuffs," I said and sheathed my sword. "I thought we'd have to restrain them."

She laughed and shook her head.

The sirens hissed. "Why isn't our song working?" the middle one demanded.

"We're soulmates to the rainbow-haired goddess up there," Jasper said. "Your siren song won't work on us."

"Soulmates!" the sirens gasped and tried to flee, but my trio were faster.

They surprised me by not killing them, but instead secured magic cuffs on the sirens' wrists.

"I was just going to net them if they couldn't catch them," Grul'ma explained and shrugged. "This is easier."

The dock master who had requested the help, was extremely grateful and paid us a little extra for bringing the sirens in alive so they could be transported far away.

"I hate soulmates," one of the sirens cried as we left. "Mortal enemies. Hate them. Curse you!"

"Well, now I know that soulmates and sirens are enemies," I said. "Why didn't you guys just explain to me that you couldn't be lured by them?"

"We did, several times," Grayson said and shook his head. "You just thought we were being cocky."

"Well, I'm glad that's over. Let's go home."

"Home sounds great," Grayson said. He headed towards the portal and called over his shoulder, "Dibs on telling Silas Nadia started a bar brawl!"

"No!" I yelled and ran after him.

Even though there were still some uncertainties about the future, I knew as long as I had them by my side, everything would work out fine.

34

BONUS: HAPPY EVER AFTER

Grayson and Jasper chased after Esmeralda, our eldest child, trying to get her to eat her dinner. Her rainbow hair cast beams of multicolored light that bounced around the dining hall as she ran away from them, ducking and sliding under tables, and through guild members' legs as they ate their dinners. The three-year-old was fast and it often took more than one of us to catch her, to corner her, when she got it in her mind that she wanted to run around. Somehow, she'd developed the ability to move faster than humanly possible, or demigodly possible, for short bursts. It reminded me of Dart a bit and I'd gone to him for advice on how to counteract it.

Thankfully, everyone in the guild was used to her antics by now and they all loved her just as much as we did, considering her to be one of us. They often took turns babysitting so my mates and I could have dates.

Vesper, our youngest child was six months old and already displaying powers, much to his fathers' delights. I was excited he was likely to be powerful, but it made raising him a bit harder. One minute he was sitting contentedly in my lap and the next he could teleport himself across the room to the basket of fruit to grab an apple.

I sighed as he teleported himself again out of my hold. Setting down my sandwich, I stood to head over and grab him.

Dart picked up Vesper and carried him to me. "It's a good thing that he loves fruits. Hopefully, he will have better eating habits than his sister."

I took Vesper and smiled at my friend. "Thank you."

He sat next to me and said, "That's what friends are for."

"I did not realize collecting escaped children was in the job description for being friends," I teased. "I'll have to remember that when you and Emily have your child."

Dart's grin turned into a huge smile. "Only a few more weeks until we finally get to meet our baby and find out whether they'll be a girl or a boy."

"Do you have a preference?" Silas asked as he sat beside me. He kissed my cheek and took Vesper out of my lap to set him on his own. He started bouncing his knee and Vesper relaxed his head back against Silas's chest while he munched on his apple.

Seeing my mates turned into such amazing fathers made me so happy. When Esmeralda had first been born, they'd been terrified and anxious constantly. They set up rotating shifts so that one of them was always awake just in case she needed something. It was adorable.

"No, I don't care. I just want them healthy and in my arms so I can cuddle them," Dart said.

"Baby cuddles and baby naps are awesome," Silas said with a nod.

Emily waddled in, her huge belly causing her to be on bedrest often. She glowed, looking like a goddess despite the swollen ankles and dark circles under her eyes. Dart rushed to her, putting a supportive arm around her back as he guided her towards our table.

"Hey, Em," I greeted.

She smiled wearily. "Hello."

"You look ready to pop," I commented.

She groaned. "Yes, please."

I laughed and Silas slipped an arm around my waist, pulling me closer so our legs were flush hip to knee. "I miss you looking like that," he whispered in my ear.

I pinched his side. "No, sir. We are done with that."

He chuckled and kissed the side of my head.

While I loved my children and I would do it again for them, I was not planning on having anymore. Two was enough for me, especially when the two I had were so hard to wrangle.

Grayson finally caught Esmeralda and carried the squirming girl back to our table. He set her on her button the seat and he and Jasper sat on either side of her.

"Eat your vegetables and I'll give you a special treat to eat while we watch the Guild Drafts," I offered.

Her eyes brightened. "Is Aunty Natasha going to be there?"

My youngest sister, Natasha, was finally taking part in the Guild Drafts and she said she wanted to join the Golden Alicorns if our guild offered her a place. Paolo had promised to offer her a place with us, but I didn't tell her that. I wanted her to get the full experience.

My middle sister, Natalie had joined the Scarlet Dragons last year. I couldn't blame her since they had been my first choice as well.

It had stung a little not to have her join us, but even though we were back on speaking terms and visited for holidays and such, she still hadn't forgiven me. She believed I had abandoned her to our father and even though Thor had done as promised and taken care of them, she had suffered for years.

Natasha had been spared most of dealing with our father thanks to Natalie, so she was far quicker to forgive me.

"Yes, Natasha will be in the Guild Drafts," I said. "Which is why I need you to finish your food or we're going to miss it."

With renewed spirit, she devoured her food, even the broccoli she detested.

Once we had all finished our meals, we headed into town where the Guild Drafts would be projected for everyone to watch.

The town was abuzz with activity, and I could hear the sounds of laughter and music from the main square. As we entered the heart of the town, we were greeted by the sight of brightly colored tents and stalls lining the streets. The air was filled with the sweet smell of roasted meats and the sound of vendors hawking their wares. I made my way through the throngs of people, marveling at the strange and wondrous sights around me. There were jugglers and acrobats performing daring feats, and magicians casting spells that made my head spin.

As we walked further into the town, we came upon the town square stage that served as the centerpiece of the festival. The stage was adorned with banners and ribbons representing the guilds in the town, and the courtyard was filled with people dancing and singing while they waited for the Guild Drafts to begin.

Jasper grabbed my hand and pulled me forward to join in the revelry, dancing with the other festival-goers.

We spun around the dancing area, my hair glowing due to my excitement, casting rainbows all around us.

Parker, Silas, and Grayson also took turns dancing with me, swapping holding our children and spinning me around all with wide smiles on their faces. My smile didn't leave my face the entire time we danced either.

When I raised my hand in defeat, after the tenth or so song, they led me to the bench we'd claimed to watch the drafts. Jasper handed me a mug of water, which I took with a grateful smile. My mates were always looking out for my health and wellbeing, even when I wasn't.

The mayor of the town walked onto the stage, activated the magic projector, and a huge image of the stage where the Guild Drafts were taking place appeared in the sky.

Several people made appreciative noises, and I agreed with their excitement. Sometimes, magic was a truly wonderful thing.

With nervous anticipation, I watched as strangers walked onto the stage, had their magic scores displayed, and guilds raised their hands.

"It feels like a lifetime ago that that was us," Silas whispered as he held my hand, rubbing gentle circles on the back of it with his thumb.

Leaning up, I kissed his cheek and said, "A lifetime ago and a lifetime I wouldn't change."

He smiled at me, his now chin length hair brushing against my cheek as he kissed me. "You're even prettier now than the day I met you."

My cheeks heated with a blush. "Sweet talker."

"Truth speaker," Grayson said on my other side, slipping an arm around my waist to tug me closer to him. He dropped his head down until his lips were right next to my ear. "If I could go back in time, I would tell myself not to let you leave that day and take you away that instant. When I saw you behind us, all I wanted to do was grab you and kiss your gorgeous face."

Now my cheeks were truly on fire. I fanned my face. "Stop."

He kissed my cheek with a soft chuckle. "You won't be saying that word later tonight."

"Promises, promises," I taunted back.

Heat flared in his eyes and Jasper pinched Grayson's leg. "We're in public."

Grayson snarled, but whispered very quietly, "You're in for it now, mate. Tomorrow, you won't be able to walk."

"Once again, you're making promises I'm not certain you're capable of fulfilling."

"We'll see about that," he replied and turned back to face the drafts.

After a dozen or so people, Natasha walked onto the stage. In the last few years, she'd filled out with muscle and glowed with feminine beauty. There was no doubt that she'd be plagued by interested men after this day.

Her level was scanned and I felt pride sear with me at the high number that popped up.

Immediately, Paolo raised his hand. So did four other guilds.

"What is your choice?" the master of ceremony asked.

"Golden Alicorns," she replied immediately, smiling wide.

Grayson, Parker, Silas, Jasper, and I all cheered. We knew she couldn't hear us, but it was common for the guilds to cheer when someone joined theirs.

We stayed to watch the rest of the drafts, wanting to support our guild and other members, but as soon as they finished, we hurried back to the guild to greet my sister.

She threw her arms around my neck the minute she saw me and I embraced her tightly. "Welcome to the guild, Nat."

"It's so good to be with you again, sister. I've missed you something dreadful," she whispered.

"Aunty!" Esmeralda yelled and latched onto Natalie's leg.

Nat picked her up and then took Vesper out of Jasper's old. "My niece and nephew! I'm so excited to be living with you now! I'm going to spoil you rotten."

"Please don't," Silas begged.

Everyone laughed and I felt my heart expand with the utter perfection that my life had become.

I had never believed in happy ever afters, especially not for people like me. But this ... this was my happy ever after.

And I would fight tooth and nail against anyone who threatened it.

"Let's go eat cake to celebrate!" Jasper yelled.

"Cake!" Nat and I yelled simultaneously, earning laughter from my mates.

Yes, this was perfection and I would enjoy every single second of it.

Thank you for reading The Golden Alicorns. If you enjoyed this book, check out my complete fantasy reverse harem series Their Fae Goddess: http://books2read. com/QOTS

Join my newsletter for new releases, deals, and freebies: catbanks.co/newsletter